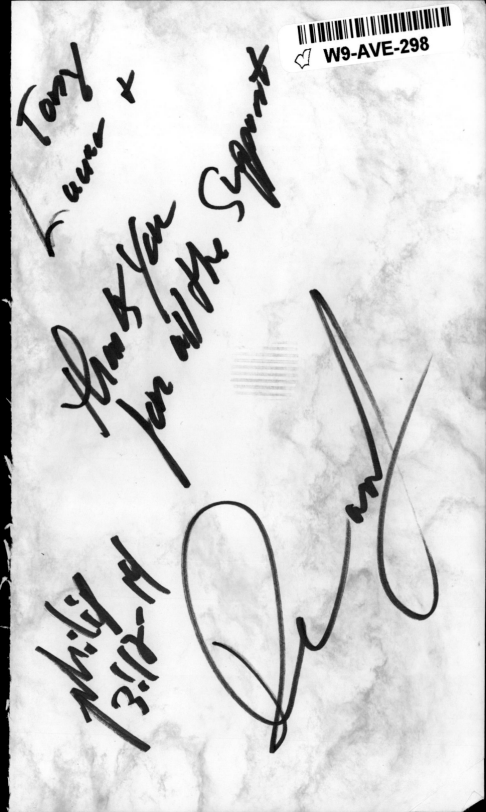

Tony
Lauren x

Thank You
for all the Support

Michael M
3:18

As I Stood At The Gate

David Woulf

As I Stood At The Gate

© David Woulf
www.davidwoulf.com

ISBN: 1890306460

Library of Congress Control Number: 2003114707

Printed in 2004

WARWICK HOUSE PUBLISHING
720 Court Street
Lynchburg, VA 24504
(434) 846-1200

Dedicated to my mother

In memory of
Lisa Laverne Vaughan
Barbara Odell Leftwich
Joseph Louis Porter
Rev. Charles "Bumper" Herndon II
Peggy Fore Harmon
All of whom have inspired and encouraged me.

CHAPTER 1

END OF SUMMER, 1965

10:00 a.m.
Saturday Morning

Matilean Johnson stood on the street corner staring at Old Man Woodson's house. With one hand twirling an extended pigtail, she spat on the other and caressed the saliva over her ashy, skinny legs. She possessed the complexion of dark mocha mixed with midnight. She adjusted her blouse and straightened her black mini-skirt. A few specks of dust had collected on the patent-leather shoes she wore only on special occasions. With a quick brush of her hand and a few wipes around the soles, the dust was gone. She wanted to look nothing less than perfect. Contemplative, once again, her gaze fell upon the house.

Old Man Woodson lived in a beautiful house at the edge of a historic district in Lynchburg, Virginia. For fifteen years he took care of the grounds of the sixteen-room house for Mr. O'Neal, a rich, white banker. The house had been in Mr. O'Neal's family for over a half century, and while other families sold their properties because of the fuel shortage during World War II, Mr.

O'Neal held on to his home. As fuel was rationed, and as it became too expensive to keep up these large homes, more families began to abandon them. Many of these abandoned homes endured seasons of bad weather and no maintenance. Realtors found it very lucrative to restructure and renovate many of these beautiful, dilapidated homes into small apartments. Working, middle-class whites moved in and occupied the majority of the apartments and single-family homes. But it wasn't until the Negro population began renting in the historic district that Mr. O'Neal, too, chose to take refuge in a white, affluent, suburban neighborhood. Rather than sell his beautiful home to the realtors, he sold the entire property to Old Man Woodson and at a poor man's price.

Mr. O'Neal was amazed by how much Old Man Woodson resembled a white man, given his straight hair, blue eyes, pointed nose, and thin lips. He became very fond of Old Man Woodson and treated him just like a brother, the brother he never had. He introduced him to friends at the all-white country club, shared many late afternoon drinks on the porch, and confided in him. It was no secret that Old Man Woodson acquired the property because of the complexion of his skin and not his labor.

Matilean approached the black handrail that ran alongside rock steps in front of Old Man Woodson's house. The rocks ended two feet in front of a beautifully wired, green gate. On each side of the gate were flower hedges that ran along each side of the house. Matilean leaned on the gate to peek around one of the hedges for a better look at the front yard. In opposite corners of the yard were two pine trees. A concrete walkway led from the gate to the bottom of the porch stairs and continued around the right side of the house. Another black handrail divided the flight of red steps that led to the porch. On each side of the steps was a flat stoop, most often used for placing potted arrangements, but sometimes used for sitting. The house had a high, black, L-shaped porch outlined with a white picket banister attached by tall, white pillars. A garden of roses, lilacs, and tulips hid the contents under the porch. The house was white with windows trimmed perfectly in green. What a beautiful house, she thought. How could black folks afford such a house?

As she stood quietly on one of the rock steps in front of the green, wired gate, she settled deeper into thought, not allowing the tears to cascade down her cheeks. She brought to mind the first time she really saw the gate; its twisted structure coincided with her mother's fears and Old Man Woodson's threats that she didn't belong there.

When Matilean and Seth weren't physically meeting, Matilean was mentally spending every minute of the day with him. It was the one afternoon when Seth didn't appear that forced her by his house. His promises encouraged her to approach his gate, and the thought of his awaiting embrace magnetized her feet to proceed beyond the boundary of the gate.

The voice of distress tested his devotion. And his family values denied her the opportunity to greet him like a beautiful, summer breeze coming in from the south. Surprisingly to Matilean, Seth's voice rushed off the porch with abrupt anxiety, and a tornado of panic blew his summer breeze off course. The truth of her status and his position was revealed at the gate on that day.

The events of that day solidified suspicions her mother embraced about fair-skinned people. For

Matilean, somehow the gate mimicked her life: iron that was forced together by a continuous twist was enough to hold the gate together; but Matilean wasn't sure of the amount of strength it would take to hold her together.

"Get offa Daddy's gate!" a voice shouted from the porch.

Matilean paid no attention because that voice belonged to a familiar foe. As she started out that morning, she had decided that no obstacle would deter her—she was on a mission. She turned her head to peek at the sun behind her. "Whew, it's gon be a scorcher," she mumbled.

A few drops of sweat ran from her neck all the way down the center of her back. It had to be settled today, she demanded to herself, slicing her index finger through the air. She couldn't take any more; the worries had damn near driven her crazy. It was just too much pressure for her to endure. Nervously, she swayed from side to side, talking to herself while steadily shaking her finger in the air.

"I got to be direct, firm, and in control," she mumbled again. "I can't let his pretty hazel eyes get the best of me. No more tomorrow or later on, it's today! That's right, today!"

Again the voice screamed from the porch, "I said get yo black hands offa my daddy's gate!"

For a brief moment she feared it might be Old Man Woodson, but then she realized the voice belonged only to Lillian, Old Man Woodson's youngest daughter.

Lillian stood on the edge of the porch and looked down at Matilean. The height of the porch allowed her to feel superior. No bigger than her bark, Lillian was small in stature and big in mouth. Silky, black hair hung below her buttocks. She favored Old Man Woodson with her thick eyebrows that met to form a unibrow. The Irish in her blood was obvious from her high cheekbones and stern chin. The two began a stare-off that lasted for several minutes.

Matilean began having doubts about being there. "No, you can't run away. You here now," she murmured.

"Girl, I know you heard me. Back offa Daddy's gate." Lillian placed her hands on her hips and then shifted her weight from one side to the other.

Matilean stared smugly. She had heard this all before from Lillian at school—running off at the mouth but saying nothing of importance.

"Whatcha doin' comin' 'round here? This ain't yo neighbahood. You know Daddy don't like yo type."

She considered entertaining Lillian's childish remark.

"And what type would that be?" Matilean asked, as she purposely placed her hands on the gate to irritate Lillian.

"You know what type I'm talkin' 'bout. Ain't no need in ackin' all dumb."

"Where is yo brotha, Lilly?"

"Lookin' for Seth, huh, and what for?"

"That's nunna yo business. Is he heah or not?"

"Oh, he's heah, but I ain't gettin'im." Lillian stepped down to the top red step. "Go on home blackie! I dun told you Daddy don't want yo kind 'round heah. You make the property depreciate."

Matilean hated that she had a low tolerance for people like Lillian. It just meant trouble. What she wouldn't give to punch Lillian right in the mouth. She figured that would shut her up, at least for the moment. She gave Lillian a false grin as if the comment had no effect on her.

"Well, you know what they say Lilly, the blacka the berry, the sweeta the juice. Ask yo brotha."

"I'll tell you what they say, 'the lighta the honey sucka, the betta the necta'."

It was obvious that Lillian was looking for a fight, and she was barking up just the right tree. Although her sweet disposition could fool you, Matilean was skilled in the art of fighting. Being the youngest of three sisters and a brother, she learned quickly. You want a fight, huh? Then I'll give you a fight, thought Matilean, as her grip tightened around the top of the gate. Her jaw imprint bulged as she bit down on her teeth. She had very little patience left for this bantering.

"Nothin' to say, spook?" continued Lillian.

"Yeah, come on out heah. I wanna tell ya in yo face." Matilean hoped Lillian would accept her offer.

"Naw, tell me from here, darkie." Lillian was no fool.

"Well, the darka the skin, the deepa the roots," replied Matilean, now waiting in retaliation. Lillian skipped to the bottom of the steps.

Yeah, come on a bit closer and you'll be in reach, thought Matilean. To Matilean's misfortune, Lillian stopped just out of reach.

"Darka the gal, nappia the hair," replied Lillian, while rolling her eyes.

"Lilly, you gon always be a runner-up to me. You nothin' but half-breed, white trash. You hate the fact that this dark...beautiful...black skin can turn the head of the finest man. So be intimidated 'cause if you don't watch it, I might take yo man."

"No you don't, heifer," Lillian shouted. That did it! Lillian's blushed complexion had now turned a dark mauve and before she knew it, her finger was right in Matilean's face.

"That's exactly what I wanted you to do," grunted Matilean, when she grabbed Lillian's finger and pulled her closer. She frowned and then yanked a chunk of Lillian's long, pretty, black hair.

"Let go! Let go of my hair!"

With all of her strength, Lillian tried to pull away, but Matilean held on tight. Lillian defiantly screamed and yelled for Matilean to let go of her hair. Lillian didn't know enough about Matilean to say something that would send her into one of her awkward daydreams, but when Lillian's face turned with pity before softly saying, "Matilean, please don't hit me," Matilean slipped into her thoughts.

Matilean's mother was quick to say the daydreams were unnatural; she believed they made Matilean appear crazy. "It just ain't right," her mother would say, "fo a girl to be talkin' at one minute or doin' somethin', and then disappear into her mind the next minute."

The thought of what Christ would do, a phrase her mother often used, leaped out in her daydream and pierced her heart. Now was not the time for mercy, she thought. Yet, something within her inner core was overriding her thoughts and she began to loosen her grip around Lillian's hair. Lillian, however, wasn't patient enough to wait for Matilean to completely release her grip.

"Let go of me now, you Black Aunt Jemima!"

At that moment Matilean drew her fist back in the air and bit down harder on her teeth.

"BANG!"

The screen door slammed in the front of the house. Old Man Woodson and Seth scuffled onto the porch. Quickly, Matilean released Lillian's hair and they both dropped to the ground on either side of the gate. The two girls knelt in silence, their fingers laced over one another's as they clung to the gate.

Old Man Woodson ran his house like he was running a prison. He stood 6 feet 4 inches, and carried 255 pounds of solid muscle. From the stories Seth had told Matilean, she knew Old Man Woodson had to be the meanest man alive. There was never any evidence to prove otherwise. Old Man Woodson frowned continuously. His eyes were cold and menacing, frequently moving from one direction to another as he contemplated what punishment he would inflict upon the next infractor.

Seth's upper torso was limply extended over the banister, supported only by his father's firm grip around his neck. Seth's complexion went from a light red to a deep purple. Old Man Woodson wouldn't let go. Instead, he gripped tighter, cutting off more oxygen. Pounding down on his father's forearm, Seth tried to free himself from the grasp, but to no avail. Old Man Woodson's face tightened. His lips pressed into his gums and his eyes squinted with vengeance. Seth literally tried spitting out words.

"Pl...e...a...s...e. I...ccccccan'...t...Bre..."

"Ah know you can't breathe! You can't breathe 'cause Ah'm chokin' you, you damn fool!" Old Man Woodson yelled.

Finally, he pulled Seth's limp body back onto the porch. Seth collapsed to his knees, fighting to catch his breath.

"What? You tryin' to kill me?" he asked, gasping for as much air as he could. Strings of saliva hung from his mouth to the surface of the black porch.

"If dat's whut it takes," his voice still cold. "Boy, don't you eva," he stressed his words, "come in my face wid some shit like that. You see any dark women in this family?" He answered for Seth, "Naw, and will neva be if I got anythin' to say to the matta!"

Seth snorted up the remaining snot that hung from his upper lip. He lifted himself to face his father. Their physiques were identical.

"What differ does it matter?" Seth questioned, backing up after he asked.

"Whut, boy?" screamed Old Man Woodson.

Seth's disrespectful reply was enough to make Old Man Woodson's eyes cringe with anger. His big, wide hand came descending through the air. With one blow, Seth's body crashed into the banister. A second slap was in motion.

"NOOOO! Daddy," Lillian cried.

Her body was crunched into the gate and her hands clenched Matilean's. For the first time, Old Man Woodson took notice of Lillian and Matilean kneeling at the gate. Trickles of blood dripped from Seth's nose and landed in the puddle of saliva. Matilean watched as the blood and the saliva mixed on the porch floor. Without order or control, Matilean slipped into another thought. How strange it seemed to her that something as black as the porch and something as clear as saliva could still find the color of blood.

"How long you been there?" Old Man Woodson yelled, as he walked to the edge of the porch.

He stood tall like a giant and more intimidating to Matilean than Lillian could have ever been.

"Did you hea me? How long you been there?"

Lillian spoke up quickly, "We ain't been heah long, Daddy."

Old Man Woodson's attention was directed solely to Matilean. He waited for her to answer. Matilean came out of her thought in time to hear Old Man Woodson say, "You hea whut I said, gal?"

"No, we ain't heard nothin', Daddy," Lillian answered.

"Lilly."

"Yes, Daddy."

"Am Ah talkin' to you?"

She pondered a second. "Ummmm no, Daddy."

"Then speak when spoken to. Betta yet, come heah," he demanded.

As Lillian began to stand, Matilean clutched her fingers tighter. All the hurtful words spoken earlier were trivial now, as destruction seemed to lie in their path. Matilean wanted to protect her and the innocence that was underneath her cold and bitter facade.

Lillian reluctantly pulled her fingers away and walked very slowly towards the steps and even more slowly up them.

"Get in the house!" he insisted by grabbing her around the neck and spinning her towards the screen door. He never took his eyes off Matilean the entire time.

Matilean heard exactly what he said, but she was scared to answer him. If he choked his own kids, she could only imagine what he wanted to do to her neck.

"Well, gal," repeated Old Man Woodson.

At that moment, Matilean noticed a robin singing in one of the pine trees. She wondered why it sang, because there seemed to be nothing exciting to sing about. Even a caged bird with its door open wouldn't sing at a time like this.

Softly she spoke, allowing her eyes to rise to his waist and fall back to the ground.

"I didn't hea nothing, sir."

"Well, betta you did, but since you didn't, Ah'll be glad to say it again. Don't expect to be in this family. Ain't one of ya eva been in this family, and it'll be ova my dead body if one of ya eva is. Don't make no diffa nohow. Seth be goin' to war any day now. He got his papers, so whateva you plannin', get it on out yo head. And anotha thing, don't eva let me catch you pass that gate." He turned to Seth. "Clean yoself up, boy," and then he disappeared into the house, slamming the screen door behind him.

His words hovered in the air. Matilean slowly rose to her feet. She knew she would never forget that day. Matilean was proud of Seth. How she loved him for standing up to his father and for her. Never had she imagined he would do such a thing. Most of the guys she knew were childish. She couldn't afford having a boy right now; she needed a man. She needed Seth.

"I'm proud of you, Seth," she said, pausing. "It took a brave man to even think about standin' up to yo father. You actually did it. You tellin'im sho took a weight off my shoul...."

"I didn't tell'im," Seth interrupted.

"Whatcha mean you didn't tell'im? I heard you tell'im."

"Naw, you kinda heard me tell'im."

"Well, whatcha tell'im to make him darn near strangle you?"

Seth paused, his eyes in a daze. "I told'im I wanted to make you my girl."

"WHAT!" screamed Matilean.

Forget the fact that Old Man Woodson might hear her; she didn't care—well, as long as he didn't come out of the house. It had been four months now, and Matilean couldn't hide it anymore. Her once-fitted clothes were making it obvious that something was wrong. She was a virgin before Seth—life just beginning, the world at her grasp.

"Oh, Mat, I knew you wouldn't understand.

Daddy is old, and his way of thinkin' is old."

"You don't have to tell me. I heard'im."

"Well then, you should know you can't burst out with somethin' like that. It might kill'im. You got to wait til the right moment."

"I guess that wasn't the right moment, huh?" she scoffed.

"Mat, I'm serious."

"And so am I. Yo father don't even think he black. I mean, he might be light and even look white, but he just as black as me. Why he think like that?"

Seth was subjected to the belief that blood relationships firmly rooted his household and so many others similar to his complexion, and was never to be challenged. To mix with a person with a darker complexion was a violation of this belief. This was the first time Seth challenged the encumbered rules and boundaries that threatened his relationship with Matilean. Seth understood that his father's beliefs could never be aggressively challenged. He also believed that Matilean was never subjected to such things; therefore, any confrontation with his father through her eyes would appear trivial. He knew now why he didn't explain his family's customs to Matilean when he had the chance. She would never understand that manhood did not provide a stronger incentive than upholding tradition.

"It's not his fault he thinks like that. He was trained to think like that by his parents, his parents' parents. It's forbidden, Mat."

"You right, Seth. I don't understand, but my stomach ain't gettin' no smaller. You think my momma gon understand? Just the other day she told me I didn't look right. Say my stomach gettin' bigger. Say I'm gainin' weight."

"And whatcha tell'er?"

"First, I told her somethin' was wrong with my period. I been bleeding for weeks. It made my stomach bloated. She said I'm gon bleed to death. Then she looks at me all-strange and she says, 'Ain't neva see no period make a gal gain dat much weight. You mus' thank I'm crazy.'"

Seth laughed, "And what you say then?"

"What could I say? She is crazy and she is right. It's like she know, but she waitin' on me to tell'er. Seth, my momma ain't dumb even though I tell'er dumb stuff. How long you think I'm gonna get away with that lie, huh? You know once my momma find out, I'm sure to be in the streets jus' like my sista Ruby. And Ruby messed with a dark man."

From the hedge, Seth plucked a small twig and placed it between his teeth. "Aw, hush Mat, yo sista Ruby ain't in no streets."

"Well, she was til my Aunt Bobby took her in.

And Aunt Bobby got five kids, a no-good man and no more room, so who I'm gon live with? Sho can't live with you."

Matilean paused and waited for some type of reply.

Seth gave none. Instead, he continued to chew on the twig and glance at the passing cars.

"Seth... SETH! You listenin' to me?"

"Yeah, stop all that darn yellin'. I hea you. I told you, my father is old, and you heard'im. He'll die befo a dark person is ever allowed in the family."

"You mean dark or black, Seth?"

"Aw, you heard'im, Mat."

"So, Seth. Whatcha want me to do? Go up to him, like a slave to its master, 'Excuse me, Masa Woodson, Ah'm so sorry you old and half crazy, but Ah jus wanna apologize for endin' yo long tradition of excludin' dark-skinned blacks from yo blood line.' Is that what I'm suppose to do? How he gon exclude somebody black and he black. It's like he's usin' tradition to dilute the black blood out his bloodline. I don't know why, cause I gotta aunt who says if you got one percent of black blood in you then you black. She calls it the Virginia one drop rule."

"Well, Daddy's folks from Tennessee said it's always been twenty-five percent that declares you black. And Daddy says he got less than twelve percent in him, being that his parents are white and all. I heard a white man refer to Daddy as a Quadroon."

"You mean Coon, don't cha?"

Seth let the twig drop. He bit on the back of his teeth.

"Who cares if he got twelve percent or one percent in'im, that nigga black!"

"All right, that's enough with the jokes, Mat."

"No, you need to stop with all the jokes. All I am to you is a big joke and everybody's laughin'."

"Whatcha talkin' 'bout now?"

"I'm talkin' 'bout you. Yo daddy let the cat out the bag. You won't even gon tell me you was skippin' town on me. You don't care what's gon happen to me."

"I ain't skipping town on you."

"You goin' to vet-con, vet-lam."

"Vietnam, Mat."

"Well, wherever it is you goin'. I'll be heah by myself. And school just round the corner."

"I know all this, Mat. You ain't tellin' me nothin' new. I mean there's a lot on my mind, too—you being young, and Daddy and his thinkin'."

"You think this baby gonna care how old I am, what yo daddy think, or what color it is, whether it be light or dark, black or white, when it gets in this world? I'll tell you what color ita be, Seth. Ita be black, lookin' for someone to take care of it. Seth, I can't do this by myself."

She tried to calm herself. She didn't want to cry. Sometimes, once she got started, she could go on for hours. She backed off the gate, turned away from Seth, and sat on the top rock step. She raised her head to take a glance, and she saw Seth standing directly over her, blocking the sun's rays from her eyes.

"What?" she asked.

Seth didn't know it, but his words cut her like a knife. Sadly, she sat on the rock, confused and lonely.

Seth placed his hand on her back. The gesture was comforting to her, but still she felt no assurance that everything would be all right. She was at their mercy and that hurt more than any malicious words they could say. All the strange signs, awful comments, and old traditions couldn't make her desert from her only chance of shelter.

CHAPTER 2

2:10 p.m.
Saturday Afternoon

The days seemed to get shorter as Matilean's burdens weighed heavier. She once dreamt about the school dance, graduating, and college. Now, as she reflected, her fears were no longer molehills, but unmovable mountains. If she had been told that the direction of her life would be decided in the next two days, Matilean would have dismissed such notions.

She knew exactly what she expected from herself and her expectations did not resemble those of the neighborhood girls or the women surrounding her. Yet, she found herself in the same set of circumstances that birthed their reality: having a baby, then dropping out of school to support it.

The only thought in her head was that of her mother's voice saying, "You betta' stay away from dem wanna be white folks. Gal, they'll have you somewhere sinnin' or dead, and if you sinnin', you might as well be dead cause you'll be on yo way to hell."

Then it was the voice of Old Man Woodson, *"Ain't no dark person eva been in this family and it'll be ova my dead body if there eva is one."*

She did not hold to any of their warnings, which came to fruition the moment Matilean yielded to temptation and gave it the right of way to her life.

When Matilean pursued a desire to be wanted, she attracted temptation. The availability of a willing listener took her behind a twisted staircase to an old storage room underneath the auditorium. Everyday she and Seth met there and took advantage of an antique stage set and the eternal silence of a few decomposing wax figures that held their secret conversations and an act of fervor.

His seductive voice echoing off the old chipped paint drew her consciousness to his every touch. The wax figures observed the collapse of Matilean's will power as she felt the satisfaction of his sweet, pleasurable kiss, which consumed the fading knocks, screeches, and cracks found in an old storage room. There, in that deep, congested storage room, Matilean's virtue was lost.

Afterwards, she sat up and shamefully buried her face to keep the waxed smiles and frowns from convicting her of such sinful behavior. Without a sound, she slipped on her undergarments, adjusted her dress, and drew her legs back into her chest; then she shed tears of humiliation. Unknowingly, she uttered under her breath, "The wise shall inherit glory, but shame shall be the promotion of fools." It was a scripture her mother would quote verbatim when she suspected any of her children were committing sinful acts. Matilean felt she had committed the ultimate sin in the eyes of God and her being pregnant was surely her punishment.

Seth sat on one side of the rail as she sat on the other. He wasn't sure what he should say. Everything he said up to that point seemed to be wrong. Occasionally he observed her gazing face for an opportunity to break the silence. His tongue couldn't wait any longer.

"Whatcha thinkin' 'bout?"

Her eyes rolled over in his direction and then back. How could he ask such a stupid question? What else could she be thinking about?

Quickly, he apologized. "I didn't, I mean...."

"Stop, Seth," she spoke, "I'm thinkin' 'bout the things that brought me over heah, a baby, and where am I gon live and school. Too many things, Seth, for my mind to even process."

His head jolted toward the sky. What could he say that would comfort her? He knew no alternatives that would help the situation. The more he tried to think, the more it gave him a headache.

"I just need time to figure this out," he said.

"Time?" she asked cynically. "Time to go back and erase what happened? Time to listen to my mother and her prejudiced advice? Crazy as it sounds, it coulda protected me from all these heartaches, lies, sleepless nights, and a baby. Time is the one thing I don't have, Seth."

Already frustrated, Seth grudged,"You talk as if it's all my fault."

Matilean drifted along with one of the streaking clouds before saying, "No, I gotta take my share of the blame."

She turned towards him and asked, "Are you scared, Seth? Are you worried for me? Because one minute you wanna protect me, and the next you don't wanna accept me."

"It's not that I don't want to accept you."

"I get it, you don't wanna accept being a father. My momma said anybody can make a baby, but it takes a real man to be a father. Now I know what she means."

"Huh, yo mother, the great Christian, has spoken again," he said sarcastically. "She always tellin' you somin'. The truth of the matter, I'm scared of a lot of things: bein' a father, goin' to war, and my daddy. I never saw myself havin' no kid."

He dropped his head, studying a pattern in the sun-baked dirt. Such things relaxed him and allowed his words to flow smoothly.

"I don't know how to be a father. I don't know where to start." Seth smirked, "I guess I already started."

She cut his smirk short with razor sharp eyes. "You plantin' a seed don't make you no father."

"I know that and I don't want to run out on my responsibilities, but what I'm gon do? I'm leavin' fo boot camp on Sunday."

"What you're doing is constantly makin' excuses."

Some parts of him seemed to accept the fact he was leaving; it was as relieving as shifting his weight from one foot to the other. He understood he had a responsibility to stay, but on the other foot, who would think he was being irresponsible because he was going to war? A man called to war had to go, simple as that. The responsibility of war and its realism conjured fears that sank him deeper and deeper into thought. He kept talking, oblivious to any of Matilean's remarks.

"I don't know what's gon happen after I leave."

"At least you know where you're goin'," she was quick to comment.

His eyes gave clarity to his thoughts of death.

"I don't even know if I'm gon make it back. I read in the paper that thousands of kids my age are dyin' every day over there."

"Why go?" her voice pleaded, and continued, "why you got to fight that war when we got a war goin' on right heah? Black folks havin' a hard time, they already killed Malcom X. And they still burning our churches, and you gon run off and fight their war? Fo what? You ain't gon have more when you get back. They gon make sure of that. Seth, I need you heah with me."

His eyes continued to follow the dirt trail now being traveled by various insects, and something as minor as two ants fighting over a morsel of food symbolized the war and death in his eyes. He thought he would soon be just like those ants. From his back pocket he pulled Thursday's newspaper.

On the front of the *Lynchburg Daily* was a large headline that read, "Bodies Will Come and Bodies Will Go" summarizing the fate of many innocent young American boys that would be slaughtered for no true cause. Underneath the picture, the caption read, *"U.S. planes begin combat missions over South Vietnam. Over 184,000 United States troops will have been committed to combat by the end of the year."*

Seth remembered the first time he saw something killed. He and several of the neighborhood boys hiked the local creek for tadpoles. It wasn't uncommon for them to hike for miles, but they usually stopped just before the slaughtering plant. They had heard of the legions of other boys their ages exploring too close to the factory and accidentally getting slaughtered— supposedly mistaken for one of the hogs.

It was Seth who suggested that they keep going. He had heard how the county hogs made good riding horses. The idea was innocent enough for a try. From the creek they approached the log fence that kept the hogs from getting out. The fascination of knuckling the pigs into the sloppy mud to fight for position momentarily numbed their sense of smell.

Although Seth was fascinated, the squealing that came from within the thin, tin walls of the factory moved him away from the others to a convenient hole that was cut out of the tin wall by rust and a continuous dripping of rainwater. He grew anxious and nervous. His right eye maneuvered around the hole until he saw one of the pigs sitting in a tub of boiling hot water.

Seth pressed his eye closer to the rusty hole, at one point laying his entire body against the tin to see what was happening. One man was holding another hog down, and another man walked up with a pistol in hand. The man holding the pig pulled a long knife from behind his back and jabbed the blade into the pig's throat. The pig jerked hard and bucked as the blood spilled from its throat. But it was the gunshot to the animal's head that sent Seth into an all out sprint. Seth's running was warning enough for the boys to give chase. It scared him so to knowingly be in the face of death and unable to do anything about it. Until now, Seth had suppressed the entire incident.

Unconcealed fright latched to his realization of war because he knew during war such situations are unavoidable. He slapped the paper with his fist and tossed it into the yard.

"You don't have to go," pleaded Matilean.

"Oh God, I might not make it back!" He drifted back into consciousness. "Mat, what if I don't make it back?"

She gently placed her hand on his shoulder, "Do you wanna come back?"

"That's a stupid question!"

"No more stupid than you havin' those thoughts. If you wanna come back, then you'll make it back." She retreated with an utterance for a desperate solution to their problem. "The question is, will I be in yo plans when you get back?"

"Mat, sometimes it's hard for me to express how I feel, but I'm gon figure somethin' out."

His reply was sufficient for the moment.

"Seth, why go?"

"Cause, I don't have a choice; I was drafted."

"So."

"So! If I don't go, I'll be put in jail, and I don't want to spend the rest of my life in jail."

"I feel like I'm in jail now," she whispered.

What was difficult for him to express was easy for her to see in his eyes; yet, it didn't prevent her from seeking a worthy explanation.

"My father served in World War II and his father before him fought for his country. So I'm supposed to be the first Woodson to coward out and run to another country like so many others? I gotta go. I gotta fight. I gotta show my father that I am a man. He expects me to."

"Seth, you can show'im you're a man by helpin' me. I need you just as much as that war."

"Listen, Mat, before I leave tomorrow everything will be resolved. I promise."

His response was intended for comfort—a promise to ease her mind and remove her uncertainties concerning the future for her and the baby. As he purposely kept from looking into her eyes, she knew it was doubtful that such words could accomplish their objective.

Somehow Matilean wished she could hide all of her troubles as easily as the sun hid itself behind a few of the passing clouds. She shut her eyes and helplessly drifted away in the shade that the clouds provided. It had captured her and temporarily removed all fears. She knew her troubles would inevitably arouse the curiosity of those around her. For the moment, she allowed herself to escape within the shadow of the clouds.

She closed her eyes and lifted her head towards the heavens and inhaled the sunshine that lingered in the air. As she pretended to caress the heavens with her cheeks, she stretched out her arms and mocked a bird that soared to the endlessness of freedom, never returning to a place so full of racism, prejudices, and consequences.

She climbed high into the sky above the clouds, trying to skim the heavens in search of a haven. Even when the screen door slammed into the wall of the porch, she refused to let go of that solitude. She held on to it and the hope that some miracle would prevail and liberate her.

Was she too young to know or even realize that such an act of fervor would have such gravity? The thought of such gravity was swiftly dropping her from flight. Who would be there to break her fall, she wondered.

Matilean could hear several voices emanating from the porch. Afraid he might get exposed comforting Matilean, Seth jerked away, then quickly stood to his feet. His eyes showed relief when it wasn't his father.

Claudia, Victoria, and Ophelia, Seth's sisters, rushed onto the porch in hysteria. Even though they were cautious to mute their laughter with covered hands, a few giggles seeped from underneath their fingers.

"Shhhhh," Claudia insisted. "If you wake Daddy befo he goes to work tonight, he'll beat some black and blue on us."

The three girls danced around the porch in laughter until Claudia spotted Seth standing. She whispered in Ophelia and Victoria's ears. Again, the three muted their mouths to hold back their giggles. Each of the girls had distinct Irish cheekbones. One couldn't be certain if the genetics were from Mrs. Woodson or Old Man Woodson's side of the family, since rumor had it that the two were from the same bloodline.

Ophelia led the other two girls to the edge of the porch. Matilean heard rumors of Ophelia being undercover and sneaky. Ophelia fooled many with her fake, southern charm, which was quick to spill out an "I dos declare" or "Have mercy on me," during any conversation.

As often as possible, she swung her silky long hair that delicately flowed in layers like ocean waves over her velvet skin. She had on a pair of high shorts that exposed her long, reddish legs and knobby knees that resembled a flamingo. How she loved to prance around and strut, never yielding to any given order except Old Man Woodson's. Other than flaunting the fact that she was the prettiest of Old Man Woodson's children, she was equally delighted that Old Man Woodson's favoritism contested anyone who begged to differ.

Ophelia had a coldness that was well hidden. Often Matilean expressed to Seth that her eyes were too close together. Matilean spoke of her mother's sayings about people with close set eyes. "It was an evil that anca itself deep in a person's heart. 'Dem the ones you fear da' most cause they give the pearance of snow white, but the devil is a lurkin'."

Claudia was sharp and jagged. With a coarse raspy voice that coincided with her rough appearance, Matilean believed she had to be as rough as the roughest man. She possessed features most similar to Old Man Woodson. Her face was structured like an inverted pyramid; she appeared to have a big forehead and little to no chin. A bad case of chicken pox left scars that masked much of her beauty. Claudia's pleasure was the toughness she acquired from her father. Sure, Lillian pretended to be mean, but everyone in the neighborhood knew that Claudia was strong like an ox and to use another cliché, "as mean as a rattle snake." Since Claudia was the oldest, and since Mrs. Woodson had long given up cooking and taken on drinking, she taught Claudia through years of practice how to assume the roles of a house wife: cooking, cleaning, and even outside chores.

Over the years, the manly chores developed Claudia's lean muscle definition, which pushed defiantly through her tough skin. She wore her hair in a mushroom bob, no make up, and a pair of blue knickers that revealed her scarred knees that resulted from constant fighting.

With her arms gradually lowering, Matilean could feel their eyes stabbing her in the back. Before she could say anything, Seth was already shouting, "Don't come out here with none of that foolishness, you hea?"

Matilean made her way to her feet but refused to face her adversaries. There were more important things on her mind than them. She, however, listened with an inquisitive ear.

"Well, Brotha," cooed Ophelia. Sometimes those who knew Seth referred to him as Brother. Stylishly, with a dangled wrist, Ophelia pointed her index finger towards Seth. "Why on earth are you screaming at your siblings in such a tone of voice? Now, you don't want to give yo neighbors the impression you don't like us, do ya?" With one step, Ophelia covered a large portion of the porch. She held her chin high and with a patented extended neck, she sashayed back and forth along the porch.

"Are we embarrassing you, Brotha?" A derisive tone accompanied her question.

"Naw, but better you know, I don't feel like bein' the center of yo amusement."

"On the contrary, it isn't you that we find amusing," she snickered, then whisked her head around for affirmation from Claudia and Victoria.

"Maybe it's the way the sun has cast a shadow that doesn't match the frame of yo body," Claudia said hatefully.

As Matilean lowered her arms completely, she turned to face the girls. With sudden realization,

Ophelia exploded with drama, "Well, Claudia, what on earth are you talking 'bout?" She looked towards the sky, then continued, "I dos declare, that's no shadow—that's Matilean."

The girls burst into uncontrolled laughter.

"Sugar, you need to get out of that sun or it's sure to ruin yo skin." She paused as having gained new insight. "Then again, you're dark enough to provide yo own shade."

Claudia was the first to attempt to contain the situation when it appeared that the only reply would be that of silence. In receding laughter, "That's enough, Ophelia."

If this was a test to see if Matilean would break and retaliate, it was affecting Seth more than her. His scrunched facial expression indicated how firmly he gripped the iron rail. Matilean placed her hand on his and gently squeezed, enabling him to reduce his temper and regain his composure.

Ophelia was Seth's fraternal twin but younger than Seth by two minutes, making Seth older than Victoria by twenty-five months and twenty-six minutes. The birth order was probably beneficial for Victoria since most of the badness that was being genetically passed around skipped her; however, Lillian and Biff received the remnants.

Matilean was not surprised to see Ophelia or Claudia on the porch making fun, but she was surprised to see Victoria. Victoria was a year older than Matilean, but Victoria had been held back a grade. The two girls had attended a few of the same classes. She knew that Victoria was sensitive, reserved in nature, and giving in spirit. She drew the conclusion that Victoria wasn't like any of her sisters. Matilean often thought she had to have been adopted.

Although Victoria was a Woodson, Matilean saw firsthand how cruel Victoria's family treated her at times. Besides being slightly mentally challenged, Victoria's chubby size further provoked meanness from her siblings and friends. She had such a plump anterior and a rear to match that boys would often taunt by saying, "She was the wife of Mr. Potato Head."

Unlike Matilean, who often fought back with other attacking words, Victoria would admit defeat with a downpour of tears.

CHAPTER 3

3:00 p.m.
Saturday Afternoon

Even though Ophelia had been given two orders, she was reluctant to listen. She had a tendency to push, and she would go on callously pushing the fragile line of Seth's and Matilean's tolerance. Seth was no immediate threat to her, only a lashing would come from his tongue, anything other had better be as carefully chosen as a watermelon. Ophelia knew that her daddy was her protector and he wouldn't allow a hand or a word of anger to hurt his perfect daffodil (unless, of course, he hurled it). That was Ophelia's safety net. Seth and everyone on the porch knew it, except for Matilean, who was about to return fire, when Seth ordered her to stop.

"But I ain't no shadow, Seth."

"I know, but let me handle this."

"Then handle it befo I do."

"Listen, all she wants is for you to say somethin' so Daddy will wake up, and we don't need that trouble."

"I dos declare, Matilean, you don't have to wear those old and dirty clothes. I just sent a box to the Salvation Army," Ophelia added.

Matilean's soft face suddenly looked strained. "My clothes may be old, but they ain't dirty. And it ain't what you wear but what you know."

"From where I'm standing, you don't seem to know too much—like comin' where ya not wanted."

Ophelia's attitude was encroaching upon Seth's temper. She hated Seth for bringing this dark, black girl into their personal lives to threaten what their father was trying so hard to preserve for them. How dare he, she fretted.

She wanted to expose Matilean for what she thought Matilean was, a tramp—a Jezebel looking for someone to latch on to. She sought to break Seth by attacking Matilean. That motivated her resentment, the mother of her hatred. Ophelia's hatred was so deep that darkness and vengeance reflected in her eyes. She lazily spoke with no effort to disguise her malice.

"Do I detect a tempa from yo friend?" She hesitated, "Daddy always said some stray cats are good to keep, but I am sure he won't referring to alley cats. I tell ya, they're good for only one thing—having babies." She laughed. "If you can't control your pet then you need to take it back where you found it."

Claudia joined in with more brazen insults, "Seth, I thought Momma told you that if she can't use yo comb then don't bring her home."

Even though, Matilean frowned, her family supported those same sentiments.

"A comb get through that hair?" laughed Ophelia while adding, "she's part of the snappy, nappy from the no-comb tribe." Ophelia paused to think of a final insult that would piss Seth off. Then it came to her. "Well, I didn't know you were color blind Brotha, 'cause she definitely fails the brown paper bag test."

"Uh un', them fightin' words, Seth," Matilean murmured, before attempting to step towards the gate. Seth's nostrils began to flare; he had heard enough. He pulled Matilean back and headed towards the gate.

In this family there was a hierarchy that did not consider age or argument; Seth was third in the chain of command. Claudia and Victoria had wisely stepped away from Ophelia by the time Seth reached the porch. Ophelia backed away as he approached. She believed Seth wouldn't dare raise his hand to strike her, yet there was a speck of doubt that lingered in her throat. She swallowed hard when his eyes forced her into a corner of the porch.

A series of horn blasts caught Seth's attention. A white Cutlass convertible with wide, white-wall tires pulled up in front of Old Man Woodson's house. Seth gave Ophelia a long intense stare before starting towards the car. Ophelia's brow puckered, then she burst into tears, "I'm telling Daddy," she blurted, then ran into the house. Claudia and Victoria ruptured into laughter. Matilean was disappointed that she had not given her something to really cry about.

PT Peterson popped his head from the car window "Seth!" he screamed.

"PT, what have you gon and done now?" grinned Seth, as his eyes scanned the car from front to back, occasionally checking out his reflection in the clear shine the car gave off.

"I just drove it off the show room floor." PT smiled through every word.

PT had a soothing voice and an air that was smoother than the shine on his new car. He wore a brand new pair of burgundy penny loafers and creased khakis that he accessorized with his wavy hair.

"It has red bucket seats, power steering and brakes, tinted glass, console with tack, and simulated wire wheels."

"This car is loaded," replied Seth with excitement. "How did you get it?"

"I sauntered into Burley's Motors, ran my finger down the side. I had to get it. I simply asked Burley what he wanted for it. You should have seen him, Brother; he came from around his desk and paused to take a good look at me and put his arm around my shoulder." PT grabbed Seth's shoulder and wrapped his arm around him to escort him around the car.

"Then what?" asked Seth, who waited anxiously for the completion of the story.

"Then he says, 'Aren't you Sunny's boy?' Why, yes, sir, I answered politely and white like. Then he asked, 'How is yo daddy doing these days? I haven't seen him lately.' Oh he's fine, sir. Just fine. Of course, being considerably more polite like. 'And his business?' Before I could answer, he turned to a fellow salesman to tell him my father bought his first car from him. Sure did, I replied. Then he looked at me and said, 'I would have bet my house and my dog that your father was a white man the first time I met him.' I stared at him as if I didn't know my father looked white. Then I said, you don't say. And the other salesman looked at me and said, 'He looks white, too.' I smiled. Burley then asked, 'Son, you sure you have enough money for this car?' So then he introduced me to one of the loan officers who happened to be there browsing."

"You sure are good with those words, PT."

"Don't mistake it to be the words alone, Brother. It has just as much to do with who you know as it does with how you speak. My complexion just gave me an advantage to get through the door so I was able to meet the right people. Time is slow to change, so learn to use what you have to get what you want. That's my father's saying. Until we can change the system that's what we have to do."

That was the first time Seth actually thought of the benefits his complexion offered. Now he understood why his father was so adamant about keeping to tradition. Still, parts of him knew that someone had to be the agent of change. He wasn't sure if it would be him.

Matilean happened to be listening when PT gloried in his admission of looking Caucasian. She was concerned with whether Seth would volunteer or be coerced to go along with change. One way or the other, change is unavoidable. Both Seth and Matilean knew that.

Matilean stood near the gate and watched the two bask in the sunlight over the car's appearance. PT described the other features on the car and his descriptive words lured Claudia and Victoria from the porch. Claudia purposely bumped into Matilean as she exited the gate. With a slight grin, Victoria cordially apologized for Claudia's behavior.

"That sure is a pretty car, PT," remarked Claudia. "Take me and Victoria for a ride?"

"Sure, but not right now, later. I have some important news I want to tell your daddy."

"What? You gon ask to marry Ophelia, huh?" questioned Claudia, and then spitefully looked toward Matilean.

Wonder what she's tryin' to imply, thought Matilean. Immediately Matilean responded with a roll of her eyes. The thought of marriage then dawned on Matilean as an option to her dilemma, but she knew Seth wouldn't, nor couldn't marry her. Part of her was relieved knowing that he wouldn't ask.

Why would anyone in their right mind willingly want to be in this family anyway, she considered. She looked intently in their direction, but her mind was practically engulfed in the idea of marrying Seth. Matilean deliberated to herself. Is it even conceivable under the circumstances that he would ask? No, according to her family traditions, it was more customary for shotgun weddings to be encouraged by the bride's father. And such motivation was normally a double barrel pointed in the face of a soon-to-be son-in-law. She contemplated the scene with a glare. Somehow she and her tradition failed one another.

Finally Seth's waving hand came into focus, and Matilean stood alert for his direction.

"Come heah and see PT's car."

"Why?" she remarked, "ain't it big enough to see from heah?"

Claudia threw her head in Seth's path at the mere thought of allowing anyone to speak to him in such a way.

PT slapped his hands together in laughter. "That girl sure has a tongue on her. Who is she?"

"Oh, that's Matilean," Seth said nonchalantly, as he moseyed to the back of the vehicle, pretending to be more interested in the car than her disobedience.

His course of action was intended to divert PT from any further inquiries concerning Matilean. Matilean considered the demeanor of the well-dressed

PT to be much like the luxury car—flashy, flirty, and fun. Matilean had only heard of PT once prior to his sudden appearance. She remembered Seth telling her stories about a cousin who courted Ophelia. She also remembered how grotesque it was to know such a thing and still persist on engaging in it. She used to doubt Seth's stories, but why would anyone fabricate a debauched story about their own family. She figured there had to be some truth to the matter.

PT fit the standard look it took to marry a Woodson: light complexion, straight hair, and, to top it off, his family had money. One thing Old Man Woodson liked better than a nearly white candidate was a rich, nearly white candidate. PT was a few years older than Seth, but that didn't concern Old Man Woodson as long as he didn't have to spend his own money for the wedding. The bride's father paying for the entire wedding was a tradition Old Man Woodson was more than willing to break.

Sure is a shame he's courting Ophelia, she contemplated. She offered a genuine smile as her salutation. "I apologize for sounding so rude," she added.

Claudia hastily replied, "What do you expect from those across the tracks?"

If Seth wouldn't demand respect then she would take the liberty of doing it for him.

"You're from the south side?" PT asked.

Tentatively, Matilean answered, "Yes, Capital Heights."

"Yeah! I know that area. I have lots of friends from over there. You wouldn't happen to know Bobby Tanner?"

Matilean smiled with confirmation, "You mean, Pretty Bobby?"

"That's him. I'm telling you, Seth, this boy should be a model or something. So pretty the women ask him for beauty secrets." He talked on, "How about Cookie Jones?"

"CJ? She's good friends with my sista."

Seth blurted, "How come you know so many people from ova there?"

"Half of them people are my father's customers."

PT's father was the only black florist in town. The majority of his business came from the funeral home due to an untimely death of a north-or south-side black. The majority of the families living across the south side of the tracks had a darker contrast to those few living across the north side of the tracks. This had nothing to do with longitude or latitude; rather, it was more of a deliberate attempt to isolate blacks from whites. But as more fair-skinned blacks began to move into white, working-class neighborhoods, streamlined attitudes and customs of blacks would frame and punctuate the interactions and accentuate the separation between fair-skinned blacks and darker-blacks.

Even though PT was pleasant and amusing, it upset Matilean to hear him categorize her people, his friends, and his father's customers as "them people." With considerable discontent, she wished to challenge PT and his comment; instead, she merely accepted her role and maintained silence.

From afar, Matilean noticed her reflection in the car. The height and width of her body as it was crammed into the height and width of the car door had no real resemblance to her own image. Somewhere in that dimension, she considered the rules of racism. However, the rules were not as easily distorted as her image. The rules were explicit, understood, and upheld by all, and taught to be upheld in threatening times by white people and both light and dark-skinned black people.

After the four had relished over the vehicle, they all started back towards the house.

"Ophelia sure gon like this car," Victoria gestured, while patting the hood of the car.

"Victoria, don't put yo paws on the car, you gon ruin the shine," Seth said.

"I thought I saw Ophelia on the porch as I came down the street."

Claudia supplied PT with the missing link to Ophelia's sudden disappearance.

"You did, until Brotha ran her in the house."

PT glanced at Seth, "Let me guess, her mouth?" then laughed.

They had climbed the rock steps to the front gate when Claudia angrily asked, "How can you laugh, PT?"

"Easy, I am aware of your sister's mouth. I have told her time after time to refrain from smart comments." Quickly he turned to Seth before pushing the gate open. "It was a smart comment?"

Seth nodded towards PT while Claudia argued the opposite.

"But it wasn't directed to Brotha," Claudia snapped.

Victoria attempted to play the peaceful mediator, "But you can't blame Matilean."

Claudia swiftly turned to face Victoria, "Shut up, Victoria," she insisted. Then scowling, "Blood is thicka than water and don't you ever forget it."

Matilean watched as Victoria's eyes dropped at the tone of Claudia's voice. Then Claudia turned to Matilean, expecting Matilean to give the same response.

Matilean was determined to stand her ground so she fixed her eyes on Claudia and didn't blink. Claudia outweighed her by thirty pounds, but if victory is weighed according to one's heart, then Claudia was in for a fight. With audacity, Matilean aimed her sight directly into Claudia's eyes and the two locked in a standoff. If Matilean thought the issue was settled, Claudia didn't.

Victoria was stunned that Matilean had such courage to stand up to her sister; however, she wisely disguised her excitement in Claudia's presence. PT playfully acknowledged, "Ladies, ladies, all this beautiful scenery and you two would prefer to stare passionately into each other's eyes? I am truly impressed."

Seth assisted by stepping between the two.

"G'on in the house, Claudia," Seth ordered.

Before removing herself, Claudia smirked, it was then understood by Matilean that the confrontation wasn't over—just temporarily deterred.

"Come on, Victoria," she yelled, and then stomped past PT to head up the steps and into the house.

Matilean gave a bashful smile of gratitude to Victoria before she carried out her order. No sooner than they disappeared, she closed her eyes and took a deep breath and gently exhaled.

"Are you ok?" Seth asked.

"I'm ok."

PT interrupted, "That's enough excitement for one day. But there is always a cherry on top of the sundae. Speaking of Sunday, aren't you leaving then?"

"Yeah, I gotta be at Fort Dix, New Jersey, by Monday night."

"Well, Brotha, I wish you the best. Are you coming inside to hear the news?"

"In a minute, PT," replied Seth.

"Well, it's probably better if I wait until your daddy wakes up."

"PT, that's a wise decision."

PT jogged the steps to the porch and went in the house.

They waited until PT entered the house before drawing closer to the gate. She wished Seth would forget for a moment who he was and where he was and wrap his arms around her like he did in the old storage room. Instead, Seth reached over the gate and pulled her close. She could feel the iron wires press into her side.

"Are you gon hit me?" he asked, pressing against the gate.

The wires were pressed deep enough against his chest and stomach that she could feel his body and still be considered at a safe distance.

"Why would I do that?" she asked curiously.

"I figure to release some of that built up anger."

"You think my anger extends to you or yo sistas?"

In order to satisfy her question, Seth agreed with both of her choices.

"No, Seth, it's your tradition that upsets me and the fact yo sistas would fight so hard to protect it. Why else would Claudia not like me? Why else would anyone in yo entire family not like me?"

She shook her head out of shame. His family and many like them would bemoan the loss of traditional values. Even though it was those same traditions that the white man used to crucify blacks, now blacks adopted them to crucify other blacks. One thing was certain, she was adamant not to willingly participate in such things.

"My momma says, 'If we's divided, then we's conquered.' Yet she supports division amongst white folks and between other blacks. When will we learn from what the white folk have done and from what they still doin' to all our people? I don't see the government stoppin' the KKK from beatin' and killin' us."

"Wow, where did that come from, Harriet Tubman?"

She placed her hand over her heart. "It came from here, Seth. I don't expect you to understand. The more I think about this black and white thing, I just get angry."

"Girl, you're a female Martin Luther King, Jr. Maybe he can recruit you."

"Maybe, then again, I might have preferred Malcom X since his approach got people to listen."

"Yeah, right."

"Seth, I rememba' when I first saw you. You was comin' down the hallway, walkin' proud, so distinguished. Someone might think you owned the school. And you was beautiful."

From perspective, society had yet to allow a man to be beautiful, so Seth blushed at the thought of him, a man, being considered beautiful.

"I couldn't stop myself from saying somethin' to you," she said.

Seth uttered, "Excuse me, but I approached you."

"Well, what you didn't know is I put myself in yo path to be approached. But it was our first conversation that convinced me that you was the one fo me. It had nothin' to do with yo skin tone or where you lived or how much money you had." She rubbed her hand along his cheekbone.

"During that entire conversation, Seth, you neva once mentioned tradition or what you couldn't do, just the goals you wanted to achieve. And you spoke of them with such passion. Anything that you desire to be, I wanna be a part of it, too."

"All this time I thought it was my curls."

Matilean didn't laugh. "Is everything a joke, Seth?"

"Mat, I don't have the answers. I'd be lying if I said I knew what tomorrow held. Yo guess is as good as mine."

"Then we have today. We need to take today to decide for tomorrow."

"Whatda you expect me to do, Mat?"

"I expect you to be a man. You can fight for yo country, surely you can fight for yo child. This problem just ain't goin' away."

"Yes it can."

"Huh?"

"This problem—it can go away."

"Whatcha saying, Seth?"

"I didn't wanna mention this, but...," he hesitated. He didn't know how she was going to react. "You know Mary Ann from school?"

"Not really."

"Naw, you wouldn't, she's an upper classman. Anyway, there is a doctor in West Virginia who can perform an operation to remove the...you know. I can fix it so you can see him. And don't worry 'bout the money or gettin' there. I will take care of that, too."

"Seth, I may be young, but I ain't stupid. I heard of that kind of thing. I heard it's dangerous."

"Ah, where you hea that from? Nothin' happened to Mary Ann."

"So!" Matilean pulled away from Seth. "Do you know what you askin' me to do?"

Seth scanned the parameters before lowering his voice to a whisper. "We're too young to be raisin' a kid. Didn't you say you ain't got no place to go?"

"Yeah, but."

"How can we support a baby if we can't support ourselves?"

"We try, Seth."

His hands flew in the air in agitation, "I wish it was that easy. I'm leavin' tomorrow. Damn, why you so stubborn?"

"My momma'd kill me if she found out I did somethin' like that."

"Don't tell yo momma 'cause I sure as hell ain't tellin' my daddy."

"And the church, Seth?"

"You don't even go to church."

"I've gon enough to know that what you want me to do is wrong."

She was stunned and taken aback by his proposal; she was even more shocked that Seth had it all planned out. She considered the act vicious; she studied him like she would a stranger.

"How can you ask me to do such a thing?" she asked, sniffling.

"Well, there is another option. How 'bout an adoption?"

She wiped her watering eyes before the tears could fall.

"What?"

"You know, an adoption. Once the baby is born you give it up to some mo folks to take care of it. I overheard Momma on the phone sayin' how my Aunt Kat gave up hers."

"Hers? She gave up more than one?"

"According to Momma."

"Why would she do that?"

"Who knows with Aunt Kat, she just as wild as a mustang. She likes for the cowboys to ride long and hard until she bucks them off," he laughed. "But she always likes for'em to get back on," he laughed again.

Matilean frowned and lamented the fact that Seth had reduced love to a mere physical act.

"Well hell, I don't know. I guess she won't ready for no kids," Seth assumed.

"That'll be impossible anyway."

"Why?"

"Cause my momma gon know. She always looks at me with her nose turned up, sniffin'. Honestly, she got a nose stronger than a hound dog. When Ruby got pregnant, no lie, my momma sniffed her up and down and told her she was pregnant."

"She ain't sniffed you out yet?"

"Maybe my scent ain't as strong as Ruby's."

Seth grinned at the thought of Matilean's scent.

"Well, yo momma got a strong nose or yo sista got a strong odor."

"If I look anythin' like Ruby did when she got pregnant, then I'll be bigger than a house. I know she'll kick me out."

She paused for a second to look deep into Seth's eyes. "Seth, all I got is you."

The impression of reality came back into focus.

"Then we back to my first option. If I'm not heah to help you, then what can I possibly do?"

"Seth, I don't know."

"Then, what is there, Mat, except this?" Seth inhaled deeply through his nostrils. "I'm tryin' to help."

He tried to present to Matilean a stronger reality.

"You remember what you told me you dreamed of becomin'?"

"I wanna be a lawyer."

"Why?"

"Because," Matilean paused, "because I wanna fight to remove racism from this country."

"So, you ready to throw all your dreams away? Once you have this baby, it will never happen. You will never get a chance to be a lawyer. You too young, Mat. We too young. This doctor will give us both another chance. Do you want yo life back?"

He took hold of her hand, "Think about it, it will be like a new start, baby. I can see it in yo eyes, Mat, yo dream, and you don't want to lose it."

She felt coerced to entertain the thought of seeing the doctor in West Virginia. No matter how much she didn't agree, she saw no other alternative out of her predicament. In one breath Seth had offered his only choice of support and taken her only hopes of security.

"Mat, I'm tryin' to do what's best for the both of us."

She took a deep breath and with her exhale came an uncontrollable flood of tears. She yanked her hand from his.

"You're doin' what's best for yoself," she said, while choking on tears, "and that's keepin' yo father

from killin' you or from havin' a heart attack, which
eva comes first."

"Trust me, Mat."

"I did and now I'm pregnant."

She respected his honesty and imagined that his
suggestion to alleviate the problem had to be driven
by fear. Because Seth had a way of lifting her spirits
and an even harder way of dropping them, she questioned whether his reasons for getting rid of the baby
lay with traditional responsibility or a diminished
love for her. She did not want to entertain the idea
of Seth not truly loving her, but deep within herself,
questions of acidic proportion back washed from her
stomach to her chest. Truly, he was the only thing
she wanted to hold onto, and the more she drew
closer, the more she found herself being driven back.
Why fuss and worry about what Old Man Woodson
would say, Seth's contradictions reminded her often
enough.

CHAPTER 4

4:05 p.m.
Saturday Afternoon

Seth and Matilean did not hear Eddie's 150 pound, thin physique dart from behind Seth's large frame. Eddie lived in a nearby neighborhood where the white residents refused to accept blacks of any complexion. But it didn't prevent Seth and Eddie from becoming best friends.

Eddie had no siblings so with great delight he considered Seth to be the closest thing to a brother. At times, Seth considered him to be more of a nuisance. At an early age Eddie showed signs of balding and a deep "cow lick" outlined his forehead. There was never a time that Eddie wasn't loud. He liked saying, "I'm loud for all the people who are quiet. Life's gotta have its balances."

"You're what?" he shouted.

Immediately, a startled Matilean responded louder than Eddie's greeting. Irritated, Seth hit Eddie for scaring her. Matilean grabbed her chest and felt the rhythm of her heart pulsating like a beating drum.

"Eddie, Daddy is asleep, and if he asks who's out heah yellin', I'm gon point to you."

"No, you can't do that."

"Why not?"

"Cause, yo daddy said he will shoot me the next time I came around heah with a lot of noise," Eddie said lightheartedly.

"You think he's playing?"

"No, I think he'll find enjoyment in doin' it. And I'm not darin' enough to find out."

"Then hush."

Eddie and Old Man Woodson had a love hate relationship. Most of the time Old Man Woodson hated Eddie whenever he came around, but he loved Eddie when he brought him goodies. The goodies were a way for Eddie to barter for more time around the house. Once the goodies were gone so was Eddie.

Eddie spoke to Matilean as if she wore earplugs. "Hello, and who are you?"

"My name is Matilean Johnson."

"Where you from, Matilean?"

Seth's eyes grew increasingly larger as his frustrations grew with each of Eddie's questions.

"Don't worry 'bout where she from."

"Well, what brings you by?" asked Eddie.

Hastily, Seth replied, "That's none of yo business."

Eddie leaned into the gate, carefully checked around and said softly, "Seth, you can tell me, I ain't the kind to gossip. I can keep a secret."

Silence hung in the air.

Eddie took a closer look at Matilean. "Well, I ain't the smartest fella, but Ms. Johnson, it sure looks like you been cryin'."

Seth pushed him out of the way. "She's ok, and thanks fo yo concern."

Confused, Eddie continued, "Seth! We still havin' that pint party tonight?"

"Shhhh," Seth warned.

"Pint party?" Matilean questioned.

"The family givin' me a party and everyone suppose to bring a pint of liquor."

"Yeah, Seth's going away party, everybody's gon be heah. We gon have a good time tonight."

"Oh, you havin' a party?"

"Why not? It's his last night in town befo he ships out. The boy gotta have a little fun, 'cause once he leaves, it ain't no tellin' when he gon get to have some fun. He betta have some while he can."

"Fun." Seth's head shaking implied a contradiction to the comment.

"That reminds me; I saw Sabrina and she thinkin' 'bout comin' ova. I hope she don't bring that cinnamon girl with her."

Matilean was at a loss. Frowning, she asked, "Who's Sabrina and who's Cinnamon?"

"I call her Cinnamon, cause she got a lot of layers. She's just one big fat cinnamon roll. But not Sabrina, she's borderline and recently health-approved fine. Don't have to worry 'bout catchin' a disease from her. No sir, not at the moment, anyhow." Suddenly Eddie realized Matilean was giving him some mean looks. "Not that it matters," said Eddie, hoping to shift the attention from Seth.

Her frowns didn't stop him from telling his story. Eddie leaned over and began to whisper as if keeping some great secret. "It was said that Sabrina gave this guy gonorrhea."

A puzzled Matilean asked, "What's gonorrhea?"

"The clap," Seth chuckled.

Suddenly, Eddie's face turned serious. "I don't want to say any names, you know, to protect the innocent. Anyway, after the doctor treated Daryl Chandler, Daryl gladly paid him for another visit. The doctor, confused, asked, 'Son, why you payin' me for another visit when I've only treated you once?' Daryl smiled and said, 'cause I plan on seein' her again tonight, so I guess I'll be seeing you tomorrow'."

Euphorically, Eddie grabbed both Matilean and Seth's shoulders and shook them violently, laughing loudly.

"Shut up, Eddie," Seth barked.

"Whatcha shut'en Eddie up fo? G'on, keep talking, Eddie. Sure glad you can keep a secret. You say this girl likes Seth?"

"Ah, Ms. Johnson, I was just jokin'. Ain't no harm in jokin'."

Matilean's chances of finding out the truth about Seth and Sabrina were slim to none; the truth would be discovered only if those who knew it revealed it to her, or she somehow discovered it on her own. As for Eddie's reward, Seth gave him a hard nudge to his rib cage.

"Eddie, you need to shut up befo Daddy heas you. If he finds out I'm thinkin' 'bout having a party, the only thing I'll have is his foot in my butt."

"I wouldn't be worried 'bout yo daddy puttin' a foot up your butt," Matilean said.

"As I was sayin', you don't have to worry 'bout yo father. I brought a little somethin' to lift his spirits."

"What 'bout my spirits, Seth? Don't I need cheerin' up?" Matilean puckered at the thought of Seth's auda-city.

"What do you want, Ms. Johnson? I'll be happy to get you somethin'," said Eddie.

"Shut up, Eddie!" the two of them shouted.

"What?" asked Eddie, at a loss.

"The nerve of you, Seth, to have a party. Have you forgotten about our problem?"

"That's a good question, Ms. Johnson, 'cause it's a serious problem to have a party without a stereo. But if I'm not mistaken, Seth, yo daddy got one in his den."

Eddie had obviously missed the point, but Seth answered him anyway.

"Yeah, it's in his den locked up with the television, the ice box, and the snack box."

Eddie laughed, "It's a dog-gone-shame a man can't trust his family. The man believes his own children would steal from him."

Matilean spoke quickly, "Seth, I don't believe you. So, what time is Sabrina comin' ova?"

"Damn, Seth, you let yo woman talk to you in any kinda way. You betta' put her in her place or she liable to keep doin' it."

"He ain't puttin' me nowhere! 'Sides, my place is wherever I want it to be, not where you or Seth or anybody else say it should be!" she retorted.

"Shut up, Eddie; sometimes you talk too much."

Seth wanted to change the subject. "So, Eddie, whatcha bring Daddy?"

Eddie dug into the front pocket of his sports jacket and revealed a brown paper sack. "I got'im his favorite candy, Boston Baked Beans and Lemon

Heads and..." he reached into the brown paper sack and pulled out a bottle of Country Time Whiskey.

"I don't know," Seth replied when Eddie exposed the golden top of the bottle. "Daddy's already agitated and that'll send'im ova the edge."

Normally liquor gives people a pleasant state of mind, but for Old Man Woodson, it had the opposite effect. It would be best for them all if he were at work when the whiskey took its effect.

Eddie was quick to shut off the alarm, "Don't worry, every time I give'im a bottle, it puts'im in a good mood."

Seth countered, "But you're never 'round to see the side effects."

"Hey, let's put'im in a good mood befo he leaves fo work, and he's less likely to think anything."

"Eddie, you been 'round heah for how long?"

Eddie pondered, "I always been 'round heah."

"Then why you so stupid? When you eva known Daddy not to suspect somethin'? Think sometimes, Eddie. I'm leavin' fo boot camp at 10:30 tomorrow mornin', so he already gon suspect somethin'. He'll probably take off from work just to make sure nothin' happens. You remember the last time we had a party ova heah?"

"Sure do," Eddie grinned, "I lost my virginity that night, underneath yo porch."

"Yeah, so you say, but the next mornin' the only ones underneath the porch was you and Rimy."

Seth turned to explain, "Rimy is Biff's German shepherd."

"Euuu, that's nasty. You really ain't the smartest fella, are ya?" Matilean squirmed at the thought of what possibly happened.

Eddie shouted, "It won't no darn dog. I know a woman from a darn dog."

"Then who was she?"

"I told you I was drinkin', and I can't remember her name."

"Or her face, huh?" Seth laughed.

"Screw you."

"No, screw Rimy."

Matilean blurted, "Well, Eddie, betta Rimy than a woman who slept with most every boy in the school."

Confused, Eddie asked, "Who she talkin' 'bout?"

"She talkin' 'bout Sabrina."

Eddie burst into laughter. "So if I went to yo school, she would sleep with me too?"

Matilean shook her head, "Why stop at one dog when you can have'em all."

"Seth, did she just call me a dog?"

"Shut up, Eddie, and finish sayin' what you was sayin'."

"As I was sayin', everybody and their mammies were ova heah for the last party. They trashed the house, ate all the food, left beer cans and liquor bottles all ova the yard. Not to mention some low-down-dirty butt hole left two humongous turds in Daddy's toilet."

Eddie cried out, "I got blamed for it, and I was underneath the darn porch all night."

Matilean giggled and added, "Yeah, with Rimy."

"I told you, Seth, you need to teach yo women their place!"

Matilean's facial expression suddenly changed. "His women?" she asked, then sharply added, "get it right, Eddie, there is only one. Besides, where was yo momma, Seth?"

"Drunk and passed out on the sofa," Eddie offered.

"Every once in a while Momma likes to sip."

"Sip is an understatement, gulp is mo like it. Seth's momma has a bottomless pit. I swea, the Atlantic Ocean ain't safe 'round her."

"All right, that's enough about my momma."

Seth looked at Matilean and shook his head and softly mumbled, "She doesn't drink that much."

Eddie caught him and mockingly nodded up and down.

"That's why Daddy locked the den 'cause of stuff like that."

"So, the party is on?" Eddie asked.

"I don't know right now. I'm still waitin' to see if Daddy is going to work."

"Earlier you said he was sleepin', right?"

"Yeah, he's sleepin'." Seth took a second to think, then said, "I guess he is going to work tonight."

His jubilation changed when he remembered that Old Man Woodson added another dead bolt to the door.

"Let me handle everything, Seth," smiled Eddie.

"Ok, but under one condition."

"What?"

"Don't give Daddy that whiskey."

"All right, mo for us tonight."

Eddie skipped up the steps and onto the porch, then stopped and turned.

"Oh, I saw Biff in the alley, stringing up a cat."

"Stringing a cat?" questioned Matilean.

"He's in the alley tryin' to hang Mr. Pollard's cat from a tree. If Mr. Pollard catches'im, then Biff might be hangin' alongside that cat. They say death comes in threes."

"That'll only be two, Eddie," corrected Seth.

"Nope, it'll be three, cause once yo daddy finds out, that's the end of Mr. Pollard. Let me go and say hi to Momma Edna."

Matilean said, "Seth, I'm confused. Eddie's around your age so how come he not goin' to war?"

"I don't think he can, somethin' 'bout'im being the only child. Then again it might be a mental thing. Sometimes he ain't got it all."

Seth tried to yell under his breath before Eddie entered the house, "Don't slam the door. And don't let Momma know you got that whiskey."

The moment the door slammed behind Eddie, Seth knew his mother would find out about the whiskey.

Matilean waited for Eddie to disappear before asking, "Seth, is Eddie white or black? He's pale like white folks, but I can't tell."

Seth brushed her question aside, putting more importance on what Eddie said and figured he should retrieve Biff.

Many considered Biff to be that one bad off-spring that resulted when family genes merged. However, Biff was the smartest of all his siblings and did what most children do when they wanted attention. Particularly in Biff's case that meant doing outlandish things: hanging cats; trying to derail trains; throwing rocks at moving vehicles;

flattening tires; hiding snakes in the pantry and tub; breaking into any and everything; pretending to be dead; and his favorite, watching his neighbors have intercourse while participating with unusual sound effects.

Old Man Woodson had long given up trying to understand Biff's eccentric behaviors; instead, he sought to put Biff away. Old Man Woodson's threats spawned constant conflict between Mrs. Woodson and himself. No matter what heinous act Biff might have committed, maternal love protected him and kept him out of the various sanctuaries for mischie-vous boys.

Seth touched Matilean on the hand. "I'll be right back," he said, before disappearing around the side of the house.

He headed toward the alley where he found Biff fascinated with the time it was taking for the cat to die. In the distance, Mr. Pollard could be heard calling for his cat.

Meanwhile, Matilean leaned her back against the gate and drifted with the daylight into dusk.

"What in the hell?" Seth was taken aback when he saw the cat turning in circles and jerking to free itself from the rope's noose.

Biff picked up a stick and smacked it against the cat's back. "The son-bitch won't die."

"Whatcha doin', Biff?"

"Well I'm tryin' to kill'em so I can test this theory I got."

"What theory?"

"Whether or not cat's got nine lives. I don't think they got'em, but I plan on finding out."

"Didn't anybody tell you that you can't kill a cat 'cause it do have nine lives? Let that cat down," Seth ordered. "You jus wastin' yo time."

"Well, I'm gon stay right heah till I kill all nine."

Mr. Pollard's calls began to increase in duration and frequency.

"Don't you hea Mr. Pollard calling for this cat?"

"Aw, I ain't thinkin' 'bout him; let'im call."

Abruptly the cat stopped jerking and its tongue slipped out the corner of its mouth.

"Uh oh, look Brotha, dat son-bitch dead now." He pointed to the cat's tongue, "Look at'im, Brotha. He must've used all nine lives, 'cause he ain't jerkin' back." He laughed. "You might as well call PT."

"And tell'im what?"

"Tell'im get the flowers ready 'cause this cat dead as can be."

Biff grinned in victory as if he'd killed some large game.

"You sick, Biff," Seth said, while reaching upward to untie the noose from around the cat's neck. Once again death crept into Seth's thoughts.

He lowered the cat down by the rope. It lay stiff. Biff stood over the lifeless cat then dropped to both knees. He was fascinated. He had killed many animals before, but never before did one fight so hard and long to live and then give up unexpectedly. He tapped its stomach and stretched both its eyelids open to be certain it was dead.

"Now whatcha doing, Biff?"

"Checkin' its vital signs. You got yo huntin' knife on ya?"

"Why?"

"An autopsy!" Biff explained.

"A what?"

"An autopsy!"

"Whatcha doin' that fo?"

He looked around before whispering to Seth, "'cause, I'm a secret agent from *I Spy* and it's crucial that I determine the cause of death."

Seth screamed, "You damn idiot. You are the cause of death."

"You can't be too certain! Plus, I need yo knife to prove my theory."

"Didn't you jus prove it? It's dead."

"And it didn't die easy fo sure. I got to write that in my log later."

"And I'll tell you another thing, you crazy, and you ain't no secret agent."

Mr. Pollard could see the boys from the end of the alley hovering over his cat. He quickly transformed his walking cane into a weapon.

"Wha' ya'll doin' up der?"

The sight of Mr. Pollard quickly hopping up the alley temporarily froze the two boys. All at once, the cat latched onto Biff's face and dug its claws deep into his flesh.

"Damn!" screamed Biff, "get it offa me, Brotha. The son-bitch won't let go!"

"Nope, you opened that can of worms, but one thing fo certain, it definitely got two lives," yelled Seth before running out the alley, leaving Biff to pry the cat's claws from his face.

Biff tossed the cat to the ground and took off after Seth. The two boys cut across some old pathways and hurdled a few hedges to escape Mr. Pollard and his cane.

CHAPTER 5

5:49 p.m.
Saturday Afternoon

Matilean stood silently in front of the gate, conscious of the promises she had made to herself long ago. One minute she was planning for the simple things: Sunday dinner, a math test, Spanish club and, if the money permitted, an outing to the matinee movie at the Shady Lane Theater. Now, her newest circumstance scheduled itself at every opportunity to remind her of the harsh consequences that would result if she didn't keep to her appointment in West Virginia.

She tried to escape the thought by tilting her head backwards, closing her eyes, and listening to the crickets' mellow mimicking. The soft whining took her deeper to the place she tried to resist thinking about, the place where the consequences of her actions were birthed. She quickly replaced that thought with another. It was vivid now in her mind the struggles and sacrifices her mother made to raise her brother, sisters, and her. Before her stepfather came along, she remembered her mother working long hours and complaining of cleaning piss-pans and dumping waste buckets all day. Matilean knew from her mother's bowed posture that such jobs broke her mother's spirit. Matilean shivered at the idea of becoming just like her mother. How did she allow this to happen? She was taught better. A pain jarred its way through her abdomen; quickly she constricted her stomach muscles to hold the aching of reality back from her heart. Even when her mother held down two jobs, times were hard and food was scarce on many days. She didn't want to believe her mother begged for money and food at times, but the truth of the matter was that she did. Eventually, she figured, she would drop out of school like her mother and sister and find a job that would provoke her dreams to haunt her every day.

What greater punishment was there when she kept thinking over and over again what she could have become? For the majority of her life Matilean escaped reality through her daydreams; she used her thoughts to manipulate situations and outcomes that she replayed in her head. Frankly, her mind had always been her sanctuary, regardless of what insane things people said about her unusual behavior. Before now, she placed no restrictions on her thoughts. They would come and go as they pleased. Now, however, Matilean's mind had become a jail cell, a solitary confinement. She gave her thoughts selected visitation because she knew they refused to keep out the reality of her predicament.

In the midst of conflict, she had completely lost track of time. She had been gone all day and surely her mother would be waiting with a belt and a tongue lashing as soon as she set foot in the house. Relief extinguished her temporary fears as she remembered she had notified her mother of her plans to stay over at a friend's house for the weekend. She folded her arms and reposed her hands under her armpits. A forward tilt of the head permitted her chin to slide down her chest.

Once comfortable, she soon regained the crickets' rhythm. In the rhythm of her thoughts, she understood that Seth was being taught to accept frequent verbal attacks from his family and to adopt uncaring practices with those outside of his family's sect.

Matilean shuddered at the depth of humility it would take to even attempt to change his family's thinking. For her humbleness, what would be the feedback from his family? There would be no words of gratitude, no reflections of sympathy, and definitely no invitation to the family name. In reality Seth knew this and knew that the baby wasn't an automatic birthright into his family. Though his decision seemed uncaring, Seth reasoned with this truth. To him every road to his crossroad led to a dead end. He decided that there was only one way to protect Matilean.

The hard-soled shoes that Matilean wore offered no comfort to her aching feet. Standing only brought more discomfort. So without hesitation, she slipped off her shoes and stepped over to a patch of grass, hoping to find a cool spot that would offer soothing relief to the throbbing. There weren't many things that could replicate the sensation of a few blades of grass under tired and worn-out feet, except for a good soak in warm water.

That was her mother's favorite relief. For twelve hours Sahara Francis would labor on her feet, cleaning, polishing, ironing, dusting, and preparing dinner for the white aristocrats. On any given day, her legs would swell to the size of logs. Matilean would prepare the iron washtub, handed down from her grandmother, with rock salt and warm water to aid in reducing her mother's swelling. Matilean sat at the foot of the rocking chair watching quietly as the water and salt took effect. Relaxed, her mother's eyes closed and she drifted off to sleep.

As Matilean allowed the grass to massage in and out of her toes, she thought of how easily she could fall asleep right where she was standing.

That's until Betsy Morgan sauntered up to the house. She hummed a familiar hymn that added to the sound effect of her dragging feet. Betsy, paying no attention, bumped into Matilean, "Damn, ya scared me," Betsy Morgan jumped. She quickly caught her breath with the palm of her hand across the center of her chest and continued, "I didn't see ya standin' der."

Matilean opened her eyes and emerged from the hedge.

"You can't sneak up on people like that," replied Matilean.

"Who's doin' de sneakin'?" argued Betsy Morgan.

For a brief moment the two watched as the corner streetlight flashed on and off several times before permanently fixing itself with a soft, continuous squeak. The streetlights served as an alarm for children to find their way home and for mosquitoes and moths to make their way out. Soon more neighborhood streetlights flickered on.

Betsy Morgan looked at the light. "Heah come de bugs," she complained. Her eyes fell back on Matilean, "Baby, whatcha doin' standin' out heah all alone? Dem mosquitoes will eat you alive, gal." She swatted at a few mosquitoes.

"I'm waitin' for Seth."

"Seth!" she screamed in laughter. "Well, he ain't worth no mosquito's suckin' all yo blood is he?"

"Well, ma'am?"

"Young love," she scoffed. "Baby," danglin' her index finger, "let me give ya a piece of advice. Until ya's learn dat a bird gon fly, a fish gon swim, an a dog gon chase his own tail just to lick his ass, den you'll realize dat ain't no man worth waitin' fo, baby. Ya hea? Dos like I tellya, hea? Make'im run after you."

Betsy Morgan's smile didn't reveal that two bad marriages prompted extreme bitterness towards all men. She winked before pushing the gate open. Wedged underneath her armpit was a dingy yellowish newspaper. She adjusted the paper by stuffing it tighter between her upper arm and body.

"Well baby, Ah'sa tell'im you out heah waitin' on'im. It won't be me."

Rather than pick her feet up as she walked, the old lady slid them across the concrete and complained about her breasts and back while slowly climbing her way to the top of the steps. Matilean bent over to slip on her shoes.

Betsy Morgan reached the porch, taking quick breaths to replenish the energy she had used to get there. A light brown wig lay crooked on her head. She grabbed the ends to straighten it out before saying, "My back's'ah killin' me from comin' up dem steps."

She contributed half the pain to Old Man Woodson's steps and the other to her oversized chest.

"And dees heah breasts ain't ah hepin'." She placed her hands on the outside of each breast and forcefully slammed them together, then lifted each from the bottom, hoping to give them more elevation. "Ah'sa tellin'im you out heah," she repeated. As she turned towards the door, Matilean could still hear her wailing complaints.

"Ah'm notta' bringin' myself ova heah again," she grumbled. "Life isza too short, and Ah don't wanna be dyin' on dees heah damn steps."

Matilean was tickled to hear Betsy Morgan curse. Seth's family and friends freely used such words as a part of their everyday language. She only heard continuous profanity from the men who gathered at the horseshoe pit not far from her house. She wasn't allowed to attend such events when there were so many men around, but on occasion various dirty words floated with the wind. Matilean, however, dared not repeat any of them.

The bitter Betsy Morgan had lifted Matilean's spirits and given her a new theme on living. She hoped that in time, Seth would come around to her way of thinking.

Seth and Biff came from the side of the house but stopped before approaching the gate.

"Biff, you need to get Momma to put somethin' on them scratches. And don't be disappearin' 'cause I might need you to do somethin' fo me later."

"Am I gon get in trouble?"

"Do you care?"

"Care or not care, it's still my butt on the line."

"Just hang around, ok?"

As Biff approached Matilean, she noticed the fresh scratches on his face. She couldn't help but ask, "What happen to yo face?"

"It ain't nothin', jus a son-bitch cat. But I'm gon get'im, eight mo times," he said with an evil smirk, then dashed up the steps and into the house.

Finally the outdoors grew quiet, and before Seth approached Matilean, he scanned the perimeter for any hidden enemies. Once at the gate, he waited a few additional seconds before breaking the tranquility that had taken so long to blanket the noise.

"Mat, that boy was actually 'round there hangin' Mr. Pollard's cat."

"I know, I saw his face and looks like the cat won."

"You don't know Biff; he won't give up without a fight."

"Is that right?" She considered his response.

"Now whatcha make that face fo?" he asked.

It upset her to have to plead to Seth to be a father. To some degree, it didn't surprise her. The hope of her being first on his list of priorities was long traded in for his own security. She listened to him muster excuses about why he had to go along with the previous plans for his party.

"I sure wish I could cancel this party. Much too late now, people already en route to the house," he offered as an excuse.

She sharply cut her eyes in his direction. He had to know his worthless tactics weren't fooling her.

"You not gon say anythin'?"

"What I spose to say? You gon do what you wanna do. My feelin's don't matter. The truth is, I don't matter."

The statement was meant more as a challenge to him. Seth chose to leave the challenge alone. Instead, he invited Matilean to stay for the party. That should at least show her he wasn't planning on seeing any other women.

"I don't know if I wanna stay. I told my momma I was stayin' ova Iva's house. Haven't seen Iva since early this mornin'. She probably wonderin' where I am right now."

"Didn't you tell'er where you was goin'?"

"I did, but I didn't tell'er I would be gon this long. It's dark, and I already got to walk by myself."

"You ain't got to walk by yoself. What kind of man would I be to let you walk alone?"

"Heaven forbid you let me walk by myself. Seems to me the real question is what kind of man would ask me to go to West Virginia?"

"Come on, Mat, what do walkin' you to Iva's house got to do with goin' to West Virginia?"

Scornfully, she shook her head, "You don't get it, do ya?" She retreated from their dispute, "Well, you sure walkin' me ain't gon interfere with yo plans?"

"I'm sure."

The entire mood was shaken when a sudden burst of screams poured out from the house. Ophelia was the first to hurry onto the porch and parade as usual. This time she had something to march about. A huge diamond, bigger than anything anyone on the porch had ever seen, sat on Ophelia's ring finger. Matilean compared the size of it to her mother's wedding band. While Ophelia attempted to bring everyone into her joy, a feeling of discomfort overshadowed Seth. His face was the gauge; he was getting more upset every time she modeled back and forth, swinging her hand in the air.

Matilean smiled uncontrollably for Ophelia until Seth's bewildered appearance caught her attention.

"What's wrong?" she asked, as her smile shrank.

Unconsciously, he gnawed at his nails.

"Stop bitin' yo nails, Seth, and tell me what is naggin' at you so."

Perhaps the irritation came from the fact that he couldn't provide the same excitement and happiness for Matilean. She was definitely deserving of it. Maybe it was an insistent reminder that there might be another solution to their entire ordeal, and PT, unknowingly, had presented it in such a subtle manner that it claimed Seth's sense of responsibility.

There was a repulsive glare from his eyes. Rather than accept his responsibility and the hope it could give Matilean, he shrugged his shoulders and said, "Ain't nothin'."

She stared at him suspiciously. She knew there was a correlation between Ophelia, Seth, and herself. I best leave it alone for now, she thought. She simply noted that if Seth wanted to share it, he would have.

Matilean turned her attention back to Ophelia, who had attracted a larger crowd, mainly consisting of Ophelia's family, including Old Man Woodson, PT, and Betsy Morgan. They all gathered around Ophelia and PT to offer pats of congratulations and words of encouragement on their engagement. Lillian fought her way to the front of the crowd to take a peek at the ring's flicker. She nearly pulled Ophelia's finger out of its joint to see it glisten in the night sky.

"Lord have mercy, hold on gal befo you pull my finger off."

Ophelia yanked her hand back and fixed her hand more aristocrat-like so everyone could continue to marvel over the ring's beauty.

"Is it real?" asked Lillian.

"I dos declare. You think my Pookie gon give me a fake ring?" She laughed delightfully and continued, "Silly gal, come closer and look again. See how it sparkles? Of course it's real."

Lillian came closer to the extended hand, but this time she was careful not to touch. She glared at it from all angles. She offered a lay opinion, "Yep, it's real."

"How would you know?" uttered Claudia, who wandered over and roughly grabbed at Ophelia's hand. Unlike with Lillian, Ophelia cautiously wiggled her hand loose from Claudia's grip.

"That's pretty, PT," she said with a blank expression, then headed back to the far corner of the porch.

"Pretty?" exclaimed Betsy Morgan. "Den ya need ta git yo eyes checked. Dat ring top of de line."

"As if you really know," mused Claudia.

"He bet'not bring som'in cheap ova heah thinkin' he gon give it to my baby," said Edna.

PT joined the conversation, "I wouldn't dare, Mrs. Woodson, only the best for your daughter. That's why she's marrying me. Plus, I also got her a new make-up kit."

Matilean offered a counterfeit smile. She needs it, she thought as PT wrapped both of his arms around Ophelia's waist to give her a tight squeeze.

"Now that you bought my daughter a ring, I guess I'll let you call me Momma."

PT smiled, "Thank you kindly Momma Woodson. I'm so happy, I'm going to take my darling to the drive-in tonight."

"What y'all going to see?" Victoria asked.

"We going to see the new Ursula Andress movie, 'She'."

Edna motioned with her head, "No, not tonight,

PT. They had a big race fight ova there last weekend. Let it cool off."

Matilean was mired in the genuine smile that spread from one of Ophelia's ears to the other. The ring that PT had given Ophelia laced her with a glow that camouflaged all of her coldness and bitterness. Matilean wasn't sure if the ring created such euphoria or the fact she was getting married. For that moment, PT had allowed her to feel like a princess.

Matilean drifted in thought to the time when she could have felt like a princess. She often imagined she was Cinderella and her prince would come and take her away. Until he came, she endured much of the same insults and ill treatments as Cinderella. Unlike Cinderella, Matilean received her abuse from her own sisters, who played their roles with no deviation from the fairytale stepsisters. With a half-cocked grin to represent reality and some parts of fantasy, she wondered if she had met the prince that would alleviate her many burdens.

Betsy Morgan was the first to offer a piece of advice for their marital success.

"Now, baby dos likes I tell ya, hea, only giv'a man twenty-five percent of yo heart, so whens his ass cuts out, you'll have seventy-five percent to fall back on. I know."

"You should have taken your own advice," Edna responded. "So don't be telling dat baby no mess like dat."

"Mrs. Morgan, don't worry yo pretty self, I don't plan on going anywhere," smiled PT.

"Dat's what dey all say, but you keep all 'em promises so when he go back on dem you can remind him of when he say 'em. If he don't bide by'em then leave his a..."

"Ah Betsy, stop all dat drunk foolish talk," retorted Old Man Woodson. "Let dees kids live their own life, you don lived yours."

Take your own advice, thought Matilean.

"You ole buzzard, what's wrong wit yo eyes, 'cause I ain't dead yet. And I damn sur ain't drunk."

"You darn sho look dead," mumbled Claudia, who had a sore spot for Betsy Morgan.

"Watch yo tongue ova der, gal. Dis heah grown folks talkin'."

Edna had already taken a few drinks from the whiskey bottle and she was elated that the opportunity had just presented itself for a motherly speech. Old Man Woodson growled his unwillingness to sit around and be tormented by her drunken stupor.

"Edna g'on now, no one out heah wants to hea you, except you."

She threw her hand in the air, "The Bible says 'Only one needs to convene'."

Biff snickered, "Daddy, Momma quoting from the Bible agin, she drunk."

"Mind yoself, Biff, or yo face won't be the only place you got scratches," growled Edna.

Without hesitation, Victoria uttered, "Momma, that's two or three shall gather in his name."

She stopped and looked at Victoria, "Well, yo fat tail can stand in for the other two."

"Damn," Old Man Woodson sighed.

"Dis my baby and if I wanna give'er a few words of encouragement I can," lamented Edna.

"Well you give'er whut you want, but I'm going to work. Seth, bring yoself up heah," Old Man Woodson ordered.

Seth moved from the gate and headed up the stairs.

Mrs. Woodson clutched Ophelia by both cheeks, and then began to shower Ophelia's face with spit and various leftovers that were stuck between her teeth.

"Ophelia, I want you to know, baby, you are starting on a life of love, happiness, and…," she belched, "adventure."

Biff fanned his nose and shook his head while taking off his shoes to tie them together. Meanwhile, Old Man Woodson took Seth to the corner of the porch away from everyone.

"Seth, Ah know you leave tomorrow, and Ah don't mind you havin' a few friends ova, but no party. Ah don't won't nobody in the house and definitely stay out of that back room. You hea?"

Seth envisioned the room that harbored the cool meats, drinks, and, most importantly, the stereo. Seth looked over at Eddie, who pretended to be listening to Mrs. Woodson rave. Rather, he was very conscious of Old Man Woodson's words of warning.

"I mean whut I say, Seth. If I come back heah and there's been a party, all hell gon break loose. You listen good too, Eddie."

With a quivering throat, Eddie replied quickly and loudly, "Oh! Yes sir. I ain't the smartest person, but I know when someone is itching on a butt whipping and I'm heah to tell'ya, it won't my plan."

Old Man Woodson turned his sights back to Seth, and Seth surveyed the porch. That's when he saw the brown sack that held the whiskey Eddie had earlier. It had somehow found its way into Old Man Woodson's lunch sack. Seth's forehead wrinkled.

"Keep an eye on yo momma. Make sure she gets in the house."

Somehow, while in the midst of her own speech, Edna overheard Old Man Woodson's last remark and blurted, "Well, hell's fire, I don't need nobody keepin' an eye on me. I got two eyes to keep on myself and a third eye don't none of y'all know nothin' 'bout."

"What third eye, Momma?" Biff asked, as he tugged at the pair of shoes to make sure the laces were knotted and tightly secured.

"Neva you mind, but I be watchin'. Y'all may think I don't be watchin', but I be watchin'."

"The third eye always watchin'," agreed Betsy Morgan.

Biff laughed, "It's the bird's eye she's talking 'bout."

"Huh!" Eddie replied.

Betsy Morgan blurted, "Thunderbird—if ya drink enough of dat ya'll think ya got three or four eyes, too," and fell over Edna and Ophelia in crack-belly laughter.

Old Man Woodson paused to look up, the disgust on his face signified that was all he could take.

Biff pulled again at the shoelaces. Lillian noticed his pants and yelled, "Aw, Daddy, Biff don got dirt stains on his overalls."

"Mind yo business, Lilly," Old Man Woodson was more concerned with shutting Edna's mouth.

Edna's words continued to drag on. "I ain't the child, he is," she pointed to Seth, "So he betta keep an eye on his self."

Mrs. Morgan burst into another scream of laughter.

"I know dat's right, girl. Since he suppose to be watchin' us, why don't he watch us take another drink."

Instead of Old Man Woodson entering into a long drawn out fight, he grabbed his lunch sack and gave a hateful eye to Mrs. Woodson before going down the steps. Matilean caught herself giggling uncontrollably. She admired Mrs. Woodson's courage, but was wise to bite down on her teeth to conceal her laughter as Old Man Woodson passed through the gate. Even though she hid it well, she still received an eye of warning that meant everything she could imagine, he was thinking. With that one glance, every bit of laughter she was saving to disperse after he left had suddenly dissolved in her belly.

Nonetheless, Matilean glanced at the back of Old Man Woodson's head and awarded the victory to Edna. She wished her mother could have been there to witness such an act of strength. Maybe it would inspire her mother to stand up to her stepfather and his harsh words that he used so often to describe her children and herself.

Matilean watched as Mrs. Morgan and Edna chuckled about the entire ordeal. It didn't seem to bother them any. She wanted to ask Edna when she got her strength and where she got it. One thing was certain; Edna definitely had the strength that she wanted. Matilean's chance to find her inner strength would come soon enough.

At the bottom of the rock step, Old Man Woodson turned to take a final glance at those on the porch.

From the street he yelled, "Seth, when that gal going home?"

Matilean knew she was only the object of his need to exert his authority.

"I'm getting ready to walk her to the tracks, Daddy."

CHAPTER 6

6:37 p.m.
Saturday Evening

As day turned into dusk, cotton clouds hung in the sky and soaked up the crimson red that bled for miles. The crowd watched in silence as Old Man Woodson started the engine of his 1962 coffee colored Nova. As usual, he sat for a long minute and then slowly drove off. They waited like manikins for him to pull around the corner. Lillian was the first to run to the side of the porch and spy if the coast was clear.

"Well, Lilly?" Edna asked.

"He gon, Momma."

The porch erupted into celebration.

"It's party time!"

Edna screamed over the voices, "Wait a minute, be quiet!" She singled Victoria out of the bunch. "Victoria, shut yo mouth."

Silence once again took its grip on the porch. No one knew exactly what the alarm was for, but they waited for Edna's instructions. Edna watched down the street; then, as she predicted, Old Man Woodson's car came creeping around the corner—moving steadily towards them. As he slowly drove past the house, his eyes locked in on the entire porch. No one said a thing, and their eyes seemed to follow his until his car disappeared back around the corner. Again, Lillian ran around the side of the porch to report back to Edna. Again they waited for Edna's signal before exploding into mass festivity.

"He think he slick," she murmured, "but he can't beat me slippin' or slidin'."

Betsy Morgan's falling over on Edna in loud amusement was the signal everyone needed to commence with the celebration.

"He alway doin' some ole stupid shit," laughed Betsy Morgan.

"I've been married to him fo thirty years; I wrote the book on being slick," admitted Edna.

"Yes you did," Betsy Morgan agreed. "I member that time when ya left yo bra."

"Damn it ta hell, Betsy, some stories don't need remindin' of."

Matilean tried to follow all their conversations at once. For a laugh, PT chased Ophelia around the porch.

"Leave that girl alone, PT."

"Aw, it's ok, Momma Edna; she practically my wife now."

Instead of using the conventional steps and gate to exit, Biff decided to leap over the banister and run through the front hedges to get to the street.

Instinctively Edna's head jacked-in-the box from her shoulders. "Well hell's fire, boy, have you lost yo eva lastin' mind?"

Biff stood in the middle of the street bare foot, with his shoes tied together in his hand. While Biff began to toss the shoes in the air, attempting to get

them hung on the power line, Bopeep, the neighborhood numbers runner, hurried up the rock steps.

Edna screamed, "Biff, I jus' bought dem shoes,
you put 'em on yo feet."

It wouldn't be the first time Biff paid no attention
to her screams, and it definitely wouldn't be the last.

"Biff, don't make me come out der and whip you.
Now, I don told you to stop tossin' dem shoes in the
air."

Edna's eyes crawled over to Claudia for assistance. "Go'n in the back and get me a couple of them
dogwood switches."

"Why?" Claudia asked, giving the impression
that she wasn't going anywhere without a reasonable
explanation. "You not gon beat'im. But you always
tellin' us to go and get a belt or some switches."

Much to Claudia's surprise, as well as the other
on-lookers, Edna reached over and smacked Claudia's
face with an open hand and returned it with an even
quicker backhand to her mouth.

"Damn!" cried Bopeep. "There's too much violence on this porch."

Then Edna snatched a fistful of Claudia's hair and
stood her on her feet.

"Ouch!" screamed Claudia, "you pullin' out my
hair."

The influence of pain depleted the bitter tone in
Claudia's voice, but not from her eyes. The ends of
her brow tied themselves into a knot. Matilean could
see she wanted to challenge Edna's authority, but fear
was also present.

"Now, den I tell ya to go and get me a switch?"

Claudia's face tightly frowned, and the knot in
her brow had developed into a double slipknot.

"Yes'um," she growled.

"Then what's all the mouth fo?"

"Ma, that's enough," urged Seth.

She released Claudia's hair, "Now get on 'round der and get me dem switches."

Betsy Morgan quickly balled her fist.

"Made me wanna grab the otha side of her head. Kids dees days don't know how ta talk ta grown folks. Ita shame ya gotta cuss at'em to make'em do somin'."

"Well, ain't nothin' like seein' some good discipline," joked Bopeep, as he took a drag on his cigarette.

"Mind yo business, Bopeep," replied Edna.

Bopeep pulled a pad and pencil from his upper left shirt pocket. "Just my observation, Ms. Edna, den mean no harm."

Betsy Morgan blurted, "I got somethin' ya can observe."

Bopeep took a quick look at Betsy Morgan and dragged the thought in with the tobacco smoke only to choke on the thought of what she meant by the statement.

"And gimme one of dem cigarettes," ordered Edna.

"They Winstons," replied Bopeep.

"You ain't got a Camel?"

"Nope."

"Well hell's fire, it really don't matta. Jus' gimme one."

Suddenly, Betsy Morgan sat back into the sofa and shouted, "Now Biff, ya momma don told ya to get ya butt up heah. Now dos like she tellya, hea?"

She looked over towards Bopeep, "Bopeep, give me one of dem smokes, too. That boy is tryin' my nerves. Edna, I tellya, Biff ain't comin' out that street."

"Momma Woodson and Mrs. Morgan," interrupted Eddie, "I guess y'all ain't never heard the joke, 'Whatcha call a dog with no legs?'"

"Naw. What do ya call a dog with no legs?"

"Anything you want, he ain't gon come to you. So you can call Biff all night, he ain't comin'."

Betsy Morgan had to give her advice. "Well, it's only one thing fo ya to do, Edna."

"What?"

"Cut both his legs off, den you ain't gotta worry 'bout callin'im."

Everyone on the porch roared.

"Well, give me yo numbers," demanded Bopeep. Then he looked around before whispering, "Um, where is Ophelia?"

"With her boyfriend," Lillian snapped. "She don't want you, you old enough to be her granddaddy."

Betsy Morgan screamed, "Now dat's old. Bopeep, put me down for 022, 898, and 416."

"How much?" he asked.

"The usual."

Edna handed him a dollar. "I want to play 786 and 510. I got a feelin' my number gon fall tonight."

"You been playin' dat number for two weeks and it ain't fell yet," said Betsy Morgan.

"Well, I got a feelin' it's coming tonight."

"You know, you might be right," smiled Bopeep, "I think I'll play it, too."

Finally Biff was successful. He screamed with jubilation as the shoelaces caught hold of the power line and twisted several times around the wire before gradually dangling back and forth. Biff watched with satisfaction; then impulsively he took off around the house.

Edna called out, "Aw, the hell wit'im. Jus' don't ask me for no money for school shoes. 'cause I'm gon tell you to take yo chances and climb that der pole to get yo shoes, and pray you don't mess up my 'lectric bill when yo butt get 'lectrocuted."

Victoria responded, "Well, dat's one thing you don't have to worry about, Momma, 'cause Biff ain't gettin' 'lectrocuted for nobody."

"Who asked you?" grunted Lillian.

No sooner than Ophelia appeared, Bopeep reacted, "Well hello pretty lady," he grinned. "How ya doing these days?"

"She's doing just fine, Bopeep," said PT.

"No need to get all worked up, I just speakin'. Ain't no harm in speakin', is there?"

"I know why you're speaking."

Edna looked at the two combatants, "Y'all go on with all that foolishness." She looked around on the porch before saying, "I need somebody to run to the store for me."

Betsy Morgan scanned the porch for volunteers. When none surfaced she called for Seth. Eddie and Seth had convened for a private conversation at the side of the house.

"Hey, I need a big favor," said Seth.

"Sure, what is it?"

"Eddie, this is serious or I wouldn't be askin'. But you gotta promise not to say anything."

Lightheartedly, "What, you don gon and got some girl pregnant?"

Seth stood off and gave a mystified look.

"Dag Seth, you really got somebody pregnant."

"Hold yo voice down, Eddie, you tryin' to let everybody hea ya?"

"Seth, I was only joking, but from the sound of your voice..." Eddie paused, "Who is it, Matilean?"

Eddie and Seth looked through the spaces of the picket banisters at Matilean, who listened to PT and Bopeep argue about the war.

"You're a fool," cried PT.

"Why, 'cause I refused to fight? Shid, mo like you the fool fo fightin'. Dat's the time dem crackers will let a black man do anythin'."

"Black men have done a lot and doing a lot, so what you talking about?"

"Look around ya man, what's don changed? Some man runnin' all over the country preaching peace suppose to change something? A black man still can't use dem white toilets, drink from dem white fountains, or eat a white pie from one of dem white restaurants. I tellya, let a nigga touch one of dem pies, dem peckerwoods will kill ya dead befo the crust hit yo lips. Face it, that Martin Luther King, Jr. is preachin' to a white choir that would rather have him dead befo changing their racist system."

"Man, you have no idea what's goin' on!" cried PT.

"Oh, believe me, I know what's goin' on, but brothers like you ain't smart enough to see."

"See what?"

Bopeep exhaled a large amount of frustration. "They got black men fightin' to preserve a racist culture. Think about it, PT. The only time we are even semi-American is when they need us to fight some war, but when it's all said and done we no mo safer than the enemy we fightin'. It don't matta what you do fo this country. You still a nigga. And it don't matta how much you resemble them, 'cause they know yousa nigga."

Politely, PT waited before rebutting. "It's brothers like you that messes it up for good black men trying hard to change the system."

Rudely, Bopeep interrupted, "Nawl, that's where ya wrong, it ain't the black brothas stoppin' you from gettin' ahead, it's the white man—and he ain't shamed to tell ya or show ya. Let one nigga do one thing wrong, then all niggas are persecuted for dat one nigga's actions. Usually it's dem crackers and sophisticated niggas like you dat's doin' the finger pointing."

PT butted in. "See the first thing you need to change, man, is your mind set. When you think nothing is going to change, you do nothing to make it change. If all black men and women held to that mind set then our race would have never made the strides we've already made and are making. And furthermore, we need to stop referring to ourselves with that slave appellation."

"What?" a confused Bopeep asked.

"Stop calling each other niggas. That's what they think of us, so why empower them by referring to ourselves as such a thing. And we need strong brothers like yourself to continue to support the civil rights movement."

"Support a movement that's goin' nowhere?"

"It's going somewhere and you too will benefit from it once we get there."

Matilean observed the brown-skinned man claiming his blackness and denying the war in one breath. She realized that the activities she was witnessing had no deviation from where she grew up. She witnessed men in her neighborhood arguing every day. The same issues that PT and Bopeep argued. Bopeep had introduced to Matilean that black men, regardless of their complexion, shared a universal problem and that the law of racism was subjectively applied according to an individual's race, class, and status.

"Well, I gotta go. Can't sit 'round heah and let the white man exploit me any longer," he glanced over in PT's direction. "This nigga," referring to himself, "gotta make some money."

"Exploding," screamed Betsy Morgan. "Dat's xactly what my husbands did to me."

"Exploiting," corrected PT.

Betsy Morgan then went on complaining about which ex-husband of hers was the most sorry excuse for a man.

"I tell ya what I need ta do, Edna,"

"What? What do you need to do, Betsy?"

"I need ta find me a rich old man wit ah bad cough."

"Hell, Betsy you old yoself, he might out live you."

Betsy leaned over to respond, "Put it like dis, if he got dat bad cough, I don't plan for'im ta out live me."

Edna coughed with laughter and got enough air in her lungs to say, "I know dat's right girl."

Lillian scrambled around the porch, blowing bubbles through a small opening of a plastic instrument.

"Mrs. Morgan," Lillian called. "Yo problem ain't a man with a bad cough."

Betsy Morgan sat up straight and smiled, "Well bless yo heart baby, I knows dat's right."

"Nope, yo problem is findin' a man."

Ophelia tried to capture the laughter that accidentally dribbled out from her mouth.

"Lilly g'on in the yard blowing those bubbles," Ophelia ordered with a smirk.

Lillian ignored the command and continued to run the porch with swinging arms and floating bubbles.

"Momma, call Lilly," Ophelia demanded.

Ophelia pulled PT to the opposite side of the porch so he could calm down and so she could get away from Edna and Betsy Morgan's maddened faces, and Lillian's bubble blowing.

Betsy Morgan fluffed a few passing bubbles away from her face before saying, "Put dat stuff up, gal. Can't cha see grown folk talkin'?"

It was Betsy Morgan's comment that made her words charge at Lillian. Out of spite, Lillian drew her neck back, then slingshot it forward. Out of her mouth came a bubble of clumped saliva that landed a few inches away from Betsy Morgan's feet. Betsy Morgan choked as she tried to get her words out.

"Now ya know, dat der gal shud get her ass whipped."

"Hold on Betsy, they still my children and I ain't 'bout to let you curse'em."

"Well, let me be da first to tell ya, dat child is evil. Hell ain't got to cus'em when dey already cursed."

Edna chuckled and replied, "And I had a hell of a time havin'em, girl."

Claudia returned with a handful of dogwood switches that had already been skinned and prepared for their intended purpose. Edna reached for Lillian, but Lillian was quick to escape her clutches.

Claudia maneuvered past the quick slipping Lillian to get to the phone. The guests had to be notified that the coast was clear. Meantime, Seth was informing Eddie of his plan. According to Seth, it was a plan that needed to be well calculated.

"What I'm gon say can't be repeated. Ok? I mean it, Eddie. It stays right heah." Seth's eyes tunneled downward.

"Right heah, sure," Eddie agreed.

Eddie was eager to know his part in the entire scheme.

"I need fo you to get yo momma's car. I need fo you to take Matilean to West Virginia."

"West Virginia!" he screamed. Then cautiously lowering his voice, "West Virginia? Why she going to West Virginia?"

"'cause she gotta meet a doctor."

Excitedly Eddie uttered, "She 'bout to have the baby?"

Seth was frustrated. "Do she look like she 'bout to have a baby?" Seth refused to wait for his answer, "Nawl, Eddie."

"Now dat you mentioned it, nawl, she ain't 'bout to have no baby!"

"Eddie, stop talkin' so loud."

Seth shook his head out of irritation. He knew Eddie was the wrong person to ask, but Seth didn't have another friend who had a car or the means to get a car. It wasn't until PT came from around the house chasing Ophelia that Seth got another idea. Settling on plan B, he no longer needed Eddie to carry out his plan. He called PT over to the meeting.

"Yeah, what's happ'ning?"

"Well, I got this problem, PT."

"Hold on, Seth," PT said, then turned towards Ophelia. "I'll be there in a minute, Sugar Pie, go ahead and call some people to come ova."

"This time, why don't you call some pretty girls?" Eddie replied. "Why do it always take three ugly girls to accompany one pretty girl," he added. "This ain't no circus, so why the monkeys?"

Ophelia frowned while sucking her teeth. "Well, I advise ya to tell that to Brotha 'cause the only monkey I see is standing at the gate."

She spilled her words quickly and dashed into the house before Seth could reply. Eddie laughed as Seth shrugged the comment. Seth was even more hesitant to conspire with PT, knowing that any slip of the tongue by PT to Ophelia would be devastating.

Eddie nudged Seth with the plan. "You said you had a problem, Seth?"

"Go on, Seth, tell'im," Eddie ordered impatiently.

"Leave, Eddie."

"Huh!"

"Leave, I'm gon talk to PT alone. Go ahead 'cause you drivin' me crazy."

"I was only trying to help."

"Well, hep the man by leavin'," PT replied.

PT could sense the frustration in Seth's voice and knew that something disturbing was on his mind. With his face full of disappointment, Eddie moped into the house.

Seth rubbed his forehead while pinching his eyebrows together.

"All right, Seth, Eddie is gone, so what's bothering you?"

"Well, um," he stalled on his words, "as I was sayin', um, I kinda…." He paused to stare down towards Matilean. "PT, Matilean's pregnant."

"Pregnant!"

"Shhh, PT. I don't know what to do."

"Have you told anyone?"

"Nobody but Eddie."

"Eddie?" His voiced lowered, "Why Eddie?" He realized the answer to his question. "Are you sure he's gon keep it to hisself?"

"I'm sure, but if you plan on tellin' Ophelia she sure as heck gon tell Daddy."

"A man ain't supposed to tell his woman everything."

Seth sighed with relief.

"But you sho got yoself a problem. Now, has she told anybody?"

"No."

"How 'bout her mother?"

"Hell no! You think her momma won't be ova heah now? Matilean be somewhere dead."

"I guess you got a point there. Them southside mothers don't play. So what you gon do?"

"I need yo help."

"Help to do what?"

"Take her to West Virginia to a doctor who gon take the baby."

"Take the baby?"

"Well, I heard he got that sort of equipment to do those things."

"Oh, Seth, you sure ya want to put her through that?" PT shook his head in utter disgust. "The instruments those doctors use have left girls messed up, Seth. Half of them aren't doctors, just pretending to be. They know the girl can't keep the baby, so fo them it's easy money. Are you sure he's a doctor?"

"A friend of mine had it done, so yeah."

"Seth, you know this can kill her?"

"Kill her, what do you mean?"

"I mean just what I said Seth, and if it doesn't physically kill her it sure as heck will kill her emotionally."

"What choice I got? I leave tomorrow. You know mothers like Matilean's momma; she gon put that girl out. I won't be heah to help her, or take care of her and the baby. I might not even make it back from this war."

The conversation went mute while PT thought about what Seth wanted him to do.

"Let me think about it, Seth."

"Well, don't take too long thinkin' 'cause I gotta get her there by tomorrow."

Edna squirmed in her seat and then repeated for the fourth time, "I said I needed a store run, but don't everybody say yes at the same time."

"Whatcha talkin' 'bout Edna, I ain't heard nobody say yes."

"Betsy, don't say nothin' 'cause you don had too much to drink."

Still there was no response.

"Well, I do know dis heah, if I'm still conscious den I'm still drinkin'. And it ain't gon be me dat runs to get it. Da las time I tried to run, my breasts blacked both my eyes."

Edna couldn't help but laugh. "Betsy, the only thing you eva run is yo mouth." Then Edna pointed and, with much surprise to Matilean, said, "Come heah."

Matilean turned to look behind her, figuring Edna was referring to someone other than her. Edna jabbed her finger continuously towards Matilean. It was evident that Matilean was the intended target. Did she expect Matilean to commit suicide? That's what was bound to happen if Old Man Woodson caught her beyond the gate.

Matilean looked around for someone to relieve her of such cruelty. Seth had disappeared without her even knowing. The only person outside besides Betsy Morgan, Edna, and Matilean was Victoria, whose facial expressions showed she was extremely thankful that she was not the one selected.

As Betsy Morgan sat forward, her breasts dropped between her inner thighs. She stretched her neck to clear the height of the banister, "Can da child hea? I know her sight ain't dat good, but maybe her heain' ain't so good either. Can ya hea, child?"

Betsy Morgan glanced at Edna, "Ah, dat gal can hea me."

Edna glanced over at Victoria who tried to hide in the shadow of the porch, well out of the way of the conversation. Edna easily spotted the light complexion glowing against the dim backdrop.

"What's dat chile's name?" Edna asked.

"Matilean."

"Matilean," Edna called.

"Yes'um,"

"Push dat gate open and come on up heah."

Obediently and nervously, Matilean pushed the gate open. The same gate she was told so many times to stay away from, the very same gate she was told she should never cross. After closing the gate behind her, she was overtaken with amazement. The house seemed to grow as she approached the black handrail that was centered in the middle of the red steps.

An outburst from Betsy Morgan scared Matilean back to her awareness.

"Lawd gal, if you walk any slower, Methuselah himself will return from da grave and give you a piggy back ride. Hur' up, an old lady dyin' of thirst."

Matilean tried to outwardly control her emotions, but the fear was hard to capture. She gripped the black rail and reluctantly pulled her way towards the porch. At the top of the steps, Matilean turned to glimpse at the gate, she felt the power given off from the height of the porch. Those few seconds gave her a new found sense of being and possession. She then knew what Lillian and Old Man Woodson felt when they stood at the edge of the porch and peered down at her—power. She contemplated more; maybe it was this type of power that white folks believed they possessed over black folks. And what black folks enabled them to have.

Until now, she only played with the idea of possessing such power. It felt good up there, standing high and being able to look down and see everything unfold right before her eyes. The flowers, the yard, and even that wired green gate looked so small. With one eye closed, she focused on the gate with the other eye. With the vision of one eye, she placed the gate between her thumb and index finger and crushed it. She smiled and tossed the thought over her shoulder.

Edna sat rocking in the iron chair and most of Betsy Morgan sat on the iron sofa glider. The two rocked out of sequence, while they waited for Matilean to come and join them.

Finally, Edna grew impatient. "Suga', ain't no need spendin' all yo time looking down at that gate, 'cause ain't nothing gon change, tomorrow it's gon look the same, so come on ova heah."

Regardless of what Edna meant by the statement, Matilean understood that all the crushing in the world wasn't going to make it disappear. She conjured a deeper thought, and all the protests and marches weren't going to stop some from hating others.

As Edna said, tomorrow it would be there and so would Matilean—on the other side of it. And to her, it collectively represented racist attitudes held by white America and Old Man Woodson.

Matilean decided she would adhere to her earlier decision to allow things to happen naturally. After all, this is what she wanted and she waited for a long time to be inside of Seth's domain—even if she was only there for a moment. She reflected on what her mother would have said. "Be careful what you ask fo."

She turned to face Edna. Never before had she seen her up close. She was a perfect picture of a white woman with loose, velvet skin with an undertone of reddish-brown highlights sprinkled across parts of her face. Naturally, Matilean thought, there had to be other components than just white that made up her vibrant beauty. She thought perhaps Native

American ancestry contributed to her skin's undertone. After staring a few more seconds, she looked in
another direction.

"I want ya to go to the store and pick me up a few
things."

Confused, "The store?"

"Yeah, baby, Do-Drop In. You know where Do-
Drop In is, don't ya?"

"No ma'am."

Edna glanced over in Victoria's direction.

"Well, Victoria will go with you. Lord knows I
don't want ya to get lost. Then I'll neva get my bottle
of Thunder."

"Thunder?" interrupted Matilean, who had never
heard of the word until Biff mentioned it earlier.

"Yeah, baby, I want a bottle of Thunder Bird. Just
remember thunder when there's a rainstorm and
think of a bird tryin' to keep its butt outta one."

Betsy helped with the description, "It's in a dark
green bottle wit ah gold cap. It ain't hard ta find, a
blind man couldn't miss it. While ya at it, pick up a
bag of cracklin'. I need somethin' ta keep my teeth
sharp."

Victoria bent so far forward to peek at Betsy
Morgan's teeth that she was nearly in her mouth; she
squinted her eyes and tried to focus even harder on
Betsy's teeth, but Betsy Morgan was sucking them.

Edna dug down into the top of her blouse
and pulled out a small, brown change purse. She
unsnapped the fastening clip and withdrew a
wrinkled ten-dollar bill. She held it out for Matilean
to take while she continued to search inside the purse
with her thumb and index finger. Matilean cautiously
took the money and stuffed it into her sock. Just as

Betsy Morgan was about to comment, she couldn't help but notice Victoria staring into her mouth.

"What! Are ya tryin' ta count my teeth? Far as I can 'member, der's still twenty-four of'em."

"But ain't there spose to be thirty-six?" Victoria questioned.

Betsy looked down at her shoe, "The other twelve you can pry outta ya ass."

Edna yanked her hand out of the purse, "Betsy!"

"Well ya betta tell'er som'um."

"Victoria, get outta grown folks' mouth and worry 'bout ya own mouth." Edna turned her attention back to Matilean, "Baby, did ya get dat money?"

"Yes'um."

"Well, where is it?"

Betsy Morgan eyed Matilean. "If Ah'm not mistaken, she put it in'er sock."

"Why you put it der?" Edna asked.

"Well, I don't have any pockets."

Edna thought about it. "That's gooda place as any long as yo feet ain't too smelly. Then again, I guess it won't matter none to Do-Drop. Money is money to him. It could fall in some shit and he'd still take it."

Betsy Morgan tilted her large frame back into the gliding sofa and roared with laughter.

"I knows dat's right girl. Sometimes he even smells like it; it mus' be a distant cousin of his."

Puzzled, "Whatcha talkin' 'bout, Betsy?"

"Shit! It mus' be his cousin. Just da other day, I was in da store and he com' leanin' ova da counter. I guess he called himself flirtin'; the only thing flirtin' was dat breath of his. Girl, his breath was burning my eye lashes, it smelted just like zackly."

Edna probed, "Zackly like what?"

"Zackly like his ass," she screamed in dramatic hysteria.

After Edna managed to wipe the tears from her eyes and gain some of her composure, she said to the two girls standing in front of her, "Well y'all go on now, so you can come on back, and cut through the alley to save time."

Before the two could reach the bottom of the steps, Edna shouted with urgency for them to stop.

"And pick me up a bottle of Three Sistas." She looked over at Betsy Morgan, "I almost forgot, Betsy, I must be losin' my mind."

Victoria and Matilean were at a loss. Then Victoria looked up at Edna and Betsy Morgan to ask, "Momma, what is Three Sistas?"

The two women swung their closest arms around the other's neck and roared in laughter. Eventually Edna stopped long enough to catch her breath and respond.

"Baby, the three sistas are Wild, Irish, and that sneaky Rose. I thought everybody knew them Jezebels."

Again their laughter commenced.

"Come on, Edna, let's go back in the house, I left a few homemade jars in the kitchen marinating and calling our names."

"I knows dat's right girl. Wild, Irish, and Rose," she cackled again.

Seth passed the two women as they were on their way inside. He walked over to the edge of the porch and took a seat. He noticed that Matilean wasn't at the gate so he stood momentarily to hunt with his eyes from one end of the block to the other. Where did that girl run off to? He assured himself that she'd be back. He sat back down to wait.

He stared down at the top red step that began to dissolve into black, dropped his head, and allowed his upper torso to bend forward. He thought about what he was asking Matilean to do and wondered if he was being selfish. He promised her that everything would be all right, and that she wouldn't have to worry. Deep within himself, his stomach turned with the indecisiveness to their dilemma. Seth sat there in silence while he reasoned with his decision to send her to West Virginia.

PT exited the house. He quickly noticed Seth sitting alone on the partially dark porch with his head hung between his knees, so he took liberty not to speak until he was spoken to. PT stood afar and inhaled the crisp air that was cooling the day. By the time he reached the banister, Seth turned his head to meet him.

"Hey, PT."

"How ya doin', Seth?" PT stood with his feet slightly apart and dropped his elbows to the banister to support his upper body.

Seth tossed his hands in the air.

"Same ole same ole," he replied. Then his head dropped again.

"So you still gon do it?"

Seth gave no response.

"Seth, how does Matilean really feel about this?"

"She don't want to, but she understands the seriousness if she don't do it. I tried to get'er to consider puttin' it up for adoption or in an orphanage, but she won't fo it. She says she won't be able to hide it long befo her mother notices she is pregnant. To tell the truth, I don't know of any other solution, PT."

"Do you feel anything for her?"

"I care a lot about her."

"Do you love her?"

Seth paused to force the question down his throat.

"I told her I did."

"Forget what you told her. What are you telling yoself? The way I figure it, Seth, you know yoself betta than anyone else. You'll know if ya love a woman. Because if you don't love her then don't play with her heart, man."

"I don't know. I mean she makes me feel like no girl eva made me feel, but I'm not sure it's love."

PT chuckled softly. "You never been in love, have you?"

Seth shrugged his shoulders.

"It's cool. Once you get a taste of it, boy," PT hoisted his head to peer at the stars, "it's like a hot apple pie that melts right in yo mouth."

"Right in yo mouth?" Seth said, baffled.

"Right in yo mouth. Now, yo sister is definitely my apple pie."

"I guess you don't mind rotten apples," Seth smirked.

"Maybe a few bruised apples, but not rotten. Anyway, on top of that apple pie was a cherry."

"Oh, don't tell me ya fell for that lie, too."

"Get serious, Seth."

"I'm sorry."

"I know I'm confusing ya, but let me explain. I know I love yo sister 'cause I remember one day I was just sitting around thinkin' 'bout what I would do if I lost her, or if I waited too long to ask to marry her. Seth, the thought scared me some kinda terrible."

"Well, it scares me to know she's still here, so when ya takin' her with ya?"

"Soon, real soon," he said, smiling at the sky and then looking down at the top of Seth's head. "If ya love Matilean ya can't go through with it. If ya do lov'er then why don't ya marry her?"

"Marry her?"

"Yes, marry her."

"PT, you of all people know I can't do that, no matter how much I care about her."

"Why?"

"One word—Daddy."

"Listen, Seth, if ya love her, that's all that matters. Yo father can't live yo life, and sooner or later you are going to have to face up to what you believe is right even if it defies all that yo father believes."

"That's easy for you to say 'cause you ain't marrying her. Plus, I don't see any dark skinned women in yo family."

"There are a few and I'm not saying the family has made it easy for them, but I admire their courage because they did what they believed in, not what tradition said they should do."

"PT, earlier you said if it won't fo yo complexion, it won't no way you woulda gotten that deal on the car. Now ain't that what you said? So why all of a sudden ya singin' this new tune?"

"I still feel that's true, and sadly that's the sacrifice that some pay, but still that shouldn't stop you from marrying who you truly love. When you let the right one get away you'll find yourself looking to find someone to fill her shoes. I'll be the first to tell you, it won't happen."

"I don't know, PT."

"I understand. It's not easy and the two of ya have a serious decision to make, but I promise ya this, Seth, if ya get her to do this, it's going to hurt her deep. She may even resent you for the rest of her life."

"I gotta do what I gotta do, so are ya taking her?"

A few seconds passed before PT answered. "I guess. I'll come by in the morning to pick'er up, just make sure she's ready."

CHAPTER 7

Matilean and Victoria walked in silence, being very careful to stay in separate tire tracks that marked the alley from one end to the other. The strange sounds of the gloomy and ghostly alley pulled them closer to each other. Shoulder to shoulder they walked towards the corner light that exposed the end of the long alley. The closer they got to the light the shorter and faster their steps became until they found themselves in an all-out sprint. The sounds of their feet smacking the gravel in the alley echoed, and their heavy breathing appeared to have attracted more unusual sounds. At the end of the alley, but well within the pole's spotlight, the two girls collapsed together.

"I hate that alley," Victoria complained, as she stood to catch her breath and push her hair from her face.

Matilean was amazed that Victoria could run as fast as she did since she was carrying a lot of weight. Matilean was even more thankful that Edna had not sent her alone. She would have been petrified.

"Which way?" Matilean asked, while blowing through her nose.

Victoria pointed north and the two walked in the middle of the street as they kept their shoulders connected. Matilean searched for an opportunity to ask Victoria a question without appearing to pry.

In a soft whisper, "Why do yo family treat you so?"

"What do ya mean?"

Matilean knew Victoria understood what she meant, but maybe the question was a little too personal so she apologized for asking.

"Do yo brotha and sistas pick with you fo no reason?" Victoria asked.

"Not my brotha so much as my sistas. They pick 'cause I'm the youngest and they know they can get away with it."

"And ya let them get away with it?"

"Sometimes I got no choice, they're bigger."

"But I saw the way ya stood up to Claudia. No girl and not too many boys've ever done that."

"Why is that?"

"Because she big and has a lot of muscles. I heard my daddy say she got a lot of testosterone in her system. I guess that's what makes her so strong and mean. I sure as heck would like to get enough to last me a lifetime. But I'm just a big ole fat thing."

Matilean swept Victoria's swinging arm up to her chest. "Don't ever say that 'bout yoself."

"Well, otha people say it."

"Sure, they may say it, but it's up to you to believe the things they say. Don't let'em see you with yo head hung 'cause all they gon do is continue to pick with you. That's why I fight back. I won't give'em the satisfaction of seein' me cry and you shouldn't either. So if they say somethin' bad 'bout you, go on and hold yo head up high, and if they hit you, then sock'em in the eye."

They snickered softly to themselves. Matilean's mother had given her many lectures about defending herself. When her defense wasn't strong enough, she was directed to call on her mother. She thought about Victoria's defense and she knew there would be a time when it wasn't going to be strong enough. It was kind of funny; Matilean saw Victoria as an innocent, helpless little girl seeking protection, and Matilean was willing to give what little protection she had. The thought, however, led her to the possibility that maybe no one would come to Victoria's aid when her stand wasn't strong enough. Therefore, she hoped Victoria paid her advice no mind.

Up ahead in the distance two single bulbs lit the white wooden storefront. Trails of people exited with bags of groceries and coal to heat their stoves for the coming fall. There was also a mob of people convened outside of the store. Some were talking about the day's events, some were smoking, and some were begging for a few spare pennies to buy a cheap bottle of wine. As Matilean approached the beggars, she pressed the heel of her foot hard into the sole of her shoe to feel the wrinkled money under the bottom of her foot as reassurance that the money was still there. But she felt nothing as she twisted the entire foot around in the shoe.

Victoria noticed Matilean tugging at her sock.

"What's wrong?" she asked.

"I put the money in my sock; it must be further down."

Matilean held on to Victoria's shoulder as she removed the shoe and then the sock. Matilean's body wavered back and forth until she caught her balance. She shook the toe of her sock expecting the money to fall out at any moment, but nothing came out. Matilean got nervous; somehow she had lost Edna's money. Maybe she was confused. Maybe it was in the other sock, she thought, while she slipped on the sock and shoe. She positioned herself again on Victoria's shoulder and began to check the other shoe and sock. Still there was no sign of the money.

"Where did you put it?"

"I remember puttin' it in my sock, but it ain't heah. It usually slides to the toe of my sock."

"You got a hole in yo sock?"

"No."

Matilean ran through her mind what could have possibly happened to the money from the time Edna gave it to her until the time she reached the store. Then it dawned on her.

"When I was runnin' in the alley, the money musta fell outta my sock."

"Then we need to go back and find it," Victoria suggested.

They returned to the spot where they thought they had started running. Their eyes strained just to see the tire outlines that marked up the alley. Matilean tried to bury the consequences as deeply in her as the tire imprints in the hardened mud. She knew there would be an imprint on her of some proportion from Edna if they didn't find that money. As they searched the alley, somewhere caught in the night sky, sounds of laughter, screaming, and music could be heard.

CHAPTER 8

8:00 p.m.
Saturday Evening

After the night sky had kidnapped any remaining residue of red, more people had gathered at the house for Seth's farewell party. Betsy Morgan and Edna returned to their seats with a cup of wine and a few sprinkles of ice to give the liquor its necessary chill. Light crowds of boys with bare chests and girls in hot pants and revealing bust lines congregated in front of the house. They mingled and socialized with their own cups and bottles of tonic.

PT pulled his car right up along the bank and turned the radio on high. A song protesting the war was being played. In protest fashion, everyone who defied the war thrust their drinks and fists into the air, shouted, and sang along. It was then that Katherine, Edna's youngest sister, tiptoed into the moonlit yard, through the horde of people. The bitter taste of the past began to sour the flavor of the elder's wine. They even sat back and moved their heads in closer to each other to whisper.

Katherine's eyes glanced over a few of the blushing crew-cut and bare-chested boys with their drinks held in the air. Occasionally, to encourage Edna and Betsy Morgan's gossip, she paused with a flirtatious stare and gave soft peck kisses to several of the boys. Betsy Morgan and Edna continued sipping their drinks, burning scornfully inside, because she was successful with her flirting.

"Will ya look at ya sista. She's old enough ta be der momma."

Actually, the age separations of her eight siblings ranged from the early thirties to the late fifties, therefore, Katherine, the baby, found herself just within teasing distance.

"At least she's tryin' to be somebody's momma. Already don gave away two of her kids. I know Momma rolling in her grave right 'bout now. Times may get hard but you don give yo kids away."

A tight, short mini skirt drew all of their eyes in closer, including Betsy Morgan's, who spilled half of her wine on Edna's long cotton gown.

"Now would ya look at dat?" Betsy Morgan snorted. "That sho't dress air 'bit six inches 'bove her knees. She gotta real nerve ta put dat on wit dem ashy knees showing." She looked at Edna. "Dey don' leave nothin' to da man's 'magination."

As Katherine walked by some of the older men sitting on the stoop, one of them said, "Big leg woman, keep yo dress down 'cause what you got there will make a bull dog hug a hound."

Katherine gave a warm southern, hospitable greeting when she reached the two women. Betsy Morgan solicited Biff to go in the house and get his aunt some lotion for her ashy knees. Biff obediently scattered between the bystanders and into the house. Katherine skimmed over the comment with a playful laugh.

"What brings ya out dis way?" asked Edna, whose attention was more focused on Katherine's outfit than any answer she could possibly offer.

"Claudia called and told me Seth was leaving so I had to come and see my favorite nephew off."

Betsy Morgan whispered in Edna's ear, "Mo like findin' someone to get'er off."

Biff returned with the container of coco butter lotion, and was quickly given another command to fetch a chair and a cup for his aunt.

"I'm glad he brought that coco butter," Katherine smirked, "'cause it will do good in healing those awful cracks on your lips, Betsy."

Betsy Morgan's nostrils flared. Katherine didn't give Betsy a chance to respond. She kept talking as if the comment was a goodwill gesture. "Look at all these whippersnappers," Katherine exclaimed. "Anything around here for a lady to drink?"

Betsy Morgan blurted, "If de so-called lady wants somethin' to drink den she best be knowin' she drinkin' what de' real women is drinkin'."

"We sent Victoria and some little girl to the store. They ain't got back yet," replied Edna.

The more Betsy stared at Katherine's skirt and enviable physique, the more envy mirrored on Betsy's face until she brought to light her own vibrant youth. "I tellya, when I was yo age I was built like a brick shit house."

Katherine looked at the old woman with laughter on her tongue. "What happened to the bricks? Then casually Katherine turned to Edna to ask, "Who's this little girl that went to the store?"

"A little girl from across the tracks."

Edna leaned over to hand Katherine a brown wrinkled sack. Katherine sat in the chair that Biff brought back and slowly poured herself a drink.

"I can't believe my Seth is leaving me. It feels like the other day I was changing his diaper."

"Ya mean ya know how ta change a diaper?"

Katherine ignored the comment, to discuss more important issues, she would say.

"I don't even know why we fighting this war. President Johnson just sending them babies over there to be butchered. Now he is sending my Seth." She took a swig of the wine before saying, "It's all economical and political."

"What you mean?" PT asked.

"Money and power, baby, that is what this war is about. President Johnson's got the power to avoid all this bloodshed and save lives, including those of American boys. But everybody knows wars drive the economy. No one wants this war but the politicians.

PT contested, "President Johnson is highly favored in the opinion polls, and he's doing what the public wants. It's his job to enforce peace in the world."

"What peace are we enforcing?"

"I have to agree with Kat," Edna remarked. "What about the peace over here?"

"It's a sad thing when Huntley-Brinkley Report did a news program on the Ku Klux Klan. Giving the Klan national coverage only encourages their hateful appetite."

"To me," PT said, "it lets the entire nation know that there is a problem and this group is part of the problem."

"Them and the government are the problems," Katherine blurted after taking another sip from the cup. "I read where our government is talking about sending two astronauts to walk around in space. If they got the resources to do that, surely the government can stop these acts of violence on innocent people and this war."

"Easier said than done, Kat," PT replied. "I heard a report where the defense department receives thousands of letters from the citizens on ways to end the war. Citizens actually believe dropping snakes, tacks, and itching powder is going to stop Vietcong guerrillas and end this war."

Unexpectedly, Claudia spoke, "PT, how do ya and Aunt Kat know so much 'bout what's going on?"

"We read the newspapers and..."

Katherine cut him off. She saw an opportunity that couldn't be passed up. Her eyes veered over to Betsy Morgan's direction. "Ya see, Claudia, you can't always rely on pictures to tell ya what's going on."

Without hesitation, Betsy shot back, "I gotta picture fo ya, ya face and my as...."

"Betsy, we got kids on the porch," shouted Edna.

"Well, since Betsy wants to talk about faces, if President Johnson really wanted to end the war all he got to do is send Betsy over there, she ugly enough to make anybody retreat." More laughter smacked Betsy Morgan in the face.

She didn't find Katherine's comment funny. "Oh, I'm 'bout to go ova der, but I ain't gotta go as far as Vietnam to whip somebody's as...."

"Betsy," interrupted Edna, "don't pay Kat no mind."

Katherine gave additional small talk about her health, her job, and her neighborhood while the others poured themselves a drink. Somehow the atmosphere was always pleasant and inviting when the anticipation of drinking was the topic for the day.

"Dis will hold us ova 'til dem chillen's com' back wit de real stuff."

Katherine kissed the cup with both lips and took a quick swig. The music went static and the crowd showed its displeasure. PT was leaving the porch to attend to the car radio when Katherine tugged at his shirt.

"See if you can find Seth." She slowly turned back to Edna, "So who's this girl Seth's dating across the tracks? I know Charles ain't liking none of that," she laughed and took another sip.

"They just friends and ain't no harm in havin' friends."

"Well, you don't have to tell me; I know Charles is just like his daddy and our daddy. He cares," she responded. Edna knew she was right, but the spite within her refused to give Katherine the pleasure of being right. Katherine pulled her lips and eyes tightly together to release a loud, "Ahhhh! This got some bite to it."

Growing up, Katherine always wanted to be right and she wouldn't think twice to let you know it. It was written all over Edna's moonlit face that she couldn't stand it and she would rather tell a lie to refute Katherine than give her that satisfaction.

"Well, times is changing and you can't expect our children to live der lives according to how we were brought up," Edna replied.

Katherine hurried the drink down her throat so she could comment on the statement.

"Where did that come from? If I recall, you were
the reason that Daddy shot Tommy Williams in the
butt."

"No, I wasn't."

"Stop fibbing, Edna. You couldn't stand'im."

"Honestly, I didn't care what you were doing with
yo so-called boyfriend, Tommy Williams."

It was obvious this was one of those delicate situations that never got resolved. Instead it was closed in
a box and stored far back in the attics of their minds.
Now, however, alcohol motivated each to express
what they had been waiting to unpack for years.

"Edna," Katherine began, "I can't believe you can
sit there with a straight face and say you didn't get
Tommy Williams, who happened to be darker than
any of Mom's Virginia blueberry pies, shot right in his
butt. I know you got him shot because the next morning you asked me how Tommy was doing. Not once
had you ever asked me how Tommy was doing."

Edna turned to Betsy Morgan to explain the story.
Meanwhile the dispute had attracted Lillian, Ophelia,
Claudia and a few of their friends. Betsy Morgan listened with smiles. Then she twisted the paper tighter
around the neck of the bottle and placed it back on
the floor underneath the sofa.

"Well, me, Monica, Nadine, Pauline, and
Katherine shared a room together and all the boys
shared a room. Momma and Daddy gave us the
largest bedroom because it was more girls than boys,
and the vent in our room was directly over the wood
stove. It was around fall."

"No," Katherine interrupted. "It was still summer
because the trees were still full with leaves and they
hadn't started to change."

"But it was cold for this particular time of the year," Edna acknowledged and then continued. "Anyway, I noticed that every night an owl would show up at the same time in a tree outside of our window to wail out its normal three *hoos*. It happened for 'bout a week. After its three wails, Kat would get up around that same time to go to the bathroom. No one thought anything of it, and I personally thought Kat had come down with a weak bladder."

"You a lie and truth ain't in ya," Katherine blurted before she took another sip.

"Dog-on-it," Betsy Morgan blurted, "can you let her finish da story?" Edna waved Katherine off and then continued with her story.

"But one night Momma got real sick and Daddy made us switch rooms so Momma could be in the room with the vent. Well, around 1:30 in the morning, this owl began *hooing*. Around 2:00 a.m. it began *hooing* louder. By this time, Daddy had already decided he was gon kill the damn bird for keeping him up all night, so he grabbed his shotgun, snuck ova to the window and slowly raised it. Now I remind you that there was not a moon in sight, so it was really dark out. Daddy pointed his gun towards the tree where the *hooing* was coming from. Tommy, thinking it was Kat, *hooed* once again. Still that wasn't enough for Daddy to get an aim on him. So Daddy *hooed* back and Tommy *hooed* back to Daddy and this went on for three or four minutes or mo. Finally, Tommy had got so pissed that when Daddy said *hoo* again, Tommy screamed out, 'Kat, that's who,' Daddy yelled, 'I'll be damned.' Then, Tommy at a complete loss said, 'Who you?' with his eyes opened wide enough for Daddy to see the white around his pupils. 'Yo black ass, that's who,' yelled Daddy. While Tommy scampered out of the tree Daddy shot a buckshot in one of Tommy's butt cheeks."

The entire porch screamed in laughter.

Betsy Morgan was laughing so hard she could barely get her words out, "I guess ya don't need a full moon ta see half uh black ass blown off, it's enough white meat ta light up ah field."

"Enough for Daddy to shoot him in the other cheek," Edna added.

Even Katherine couldn't hold back the laughter as she slapped her knee with her hand and finished the last of her wine. "Lawd, when I think about it, that boy somewhere runnin' 'round with no ass at all."

PT managed to make his way through the crowd, onto the porch.

"What's so funny up here?"

Katherine withdrew her laughter, "Nothing, baby. Did you see Seth? I been here for more than an hour and still haven't seen my nephew."

"You ain't been heah fo no hour; see how she lie?" declared Betsy Morgan.

PT looked at Betsy Morgan for a split second and then to Katherine and said, "He's somewhere around here looking for Biff."

Katherine's face filled with a load of sympathy for Seth. "Biff was just here. He'll be looking all night," she replied, while wiping the mist from her eyes.

She played with the empty cup for several moments until she placed it on the floor, hoping someone would notice and offer her another drink. In response, Betsy Morgan poured the last few drops into her own cup. Why not, she thought, she bought it.

"Well if I can't get drunk enough to go to sleep, I might as well drink something that's going to wake me up. Lilly, go in the house and make me a cup of coffee."

Normally Lillian would have objected, but this time she pulled herself from the porch and accepted the responsibility.

"Aunt Kat, do you want your coffee black?"

"Good heavens no, child, I don't like nothin' black but my men!"

"That's the truth," Edna sighed sarcastically.

"The blacka the betta," Katherine replied.

Betsy Morgan whispered into Edna's ear, "If dat's da case why din't she keep dem chillens of hern? I guess dey too dark so she gav'em back to der black daddy. Dem babies gon grow up not knowing who dey are."

The wine had run out and their tempers were starting to flare up. Katherine knew what the two were referring to and it pissed her off.

"Listen," she said, "I don't care what you think you know. You should refrain from any comments on stuff you really don't know nothin' about. You just two old hags sitting around gossiping all day."

"Whatcha talkin' 'bout, Kat?" Edna asked.

"You know what the hell I'm talking 'bout. Whispering among yoselves as if I'm some third party. If you got something to say, Edna, then say it, I'm right here."

Katherine shot a glance in Betsy's direction, offering her the same invitation. With stubborn refusal to let the subject pass, she mouthed on. "Get on my damn nerves talking about stuff you don't know nothin' about. That's why I don't come over here as it is."

Ever since Edna could remember, Katherine never took responsibility for anything, not even the pawning off of her children. Sure enough, Edna had something to say and she had been waiting for the opportunity to say it. It climbed up her chest and right out of her mouth, "Hey, don't sit up heah and blame us for yo mistakes."

"What mistakes you referring to, Edna?"

"For one, that no good Lonnie Coldpepper. If you were gon run off with something dark, you coulda had some decency about it. Did you have to pick the ugliest man you could find or was that yo way of pissin' Daddy off even mo? I tellya Betsy, I wouldn't pair'im with the bottom of my shoe.

"I know dat's right," concurred Betsy Morgan.

Edna continued, "You din't want to listen to Daddy, you had to do it yo way."

"You ain't nothing but a racist, Edna, and I refuse to select one complexion over another."

Edna replied, "Look at you fighting so hard to claim yo dark ancestral heritage, lookin' to find yo roots. You didn't like being called the descendant of a house nigga, so you went out and found the darkest field nigga you could find, and had his babies just so you could stand proud and say yo daughter and son are descendants of the true motherland. Then, what yo field nigga and his kind do when you took them ova there? Huh, what they do, Kat? They ran yo butt from ova there. Still, you keep reaching out to'em."

"You don't know nothing Edna," Kat responded, "you chose to teach your kids hate and the way of the sword. When children learn prejudice, the vicious cycle continues. It ain't enough that we are fighting a war against the white man, we have to fight it among ourselves, too. Ain't you tired of seeing our people being bit by their dogs, hit by their clubs, sprayed by their hoses, and killed by their ropes, hands, and guns? So why we got to keep fighting amongst ourselves? I agree with you, Edna, it is hard fighting to show them that the person underneath this caramel complexion is just as black as them. I know many of them don't want to accept me, and it hurts, but understand, there is a greater cause and a greater good at stake. We all have to make sacrifices."

"Why you make it yo children? You had to support yo selfish cause by runnin' out on dem. Daddy rollin' ova in his grave 'bout now."

"Shit, let him roll, he'll hit one side of that box and roll back to the other."

"Girl, you watch yo mouth on this porch!"

"Edna, you don't know how rough it is out there. All your life you had Daddy to support you and when he died, Charles absorbed your struggles. I didn't have anyone. When I left the family ya'll ousted me and I refused to give ya the satisfaction of seeing me crawl back."

"But you gave his family the satisfaction of seein' you crawl to dem."

"I did what I thought was the best for my children. Lonnie and me weren't making it."

"The best fo yo children? Kat, the best you can do fo yo children is to keep dem with you. I'll say it agin; you don't give yo kids away. Times may get rough but you gotta get tough with'em, so don't talk about no sacrifice to me. I know sacrifice; I sacrificed my dreams to help raise you and these kids. I have stared rejection in the face and took its blows and sometimes I had to crawl on my belly through the mud to ovacome hurt and pain; course you wouldn't know nothin' 'bout dat. You were too busy tryin' to be universally accepted when you shoulda been learning to use yo most commonly accepted gift—yo color."

"That's the main reason I left my children with their father, so they would learn more about their culture and become part of a generation that rejected such idiotic thinking as Plessy versus Ferguson. I want my babies to use their talents, skills, and abilities to get where they want to go in this world.

"And where you plan on bein' while they are gettin' these lessons on life?"

"Because I left my children with their father doesn't mean I will be absent from their lives. My children will help change this country."

Betsy Morgan screamed, "America change? Dat will be de day."

As usual, PT jumped right into the conversation, "America is already changing. If you picked up a newspaper you would have read that President Lyndon Johnson signed the Voting Rights Bill, and Thurgood Marshall was appointed the first Black Solicitor General of the United States."

Katherine elevated her tone, "Both are a result of continuing Civil Rights struggles. But do we really want change to come at the cost of another Bloody Sunday?" She held her audience by glancing around the porch, sporadically making contact with all of their eyes. "Still these so-called "color-blind" laws are just that on the surface, but really they're designed to exclude black citizens from voting. Yet black soldiers are fighting right now for this country, but when they return, they can't have the peace to vote without some cowardly racist trying to take their lives."

"Kat, the Voting Rights Act is the start to restoring the rights stolen by such disenfranchising laws."

"Naw, PT, the start was not some law, but the innocent lives lost just so we could get to this point. That's why I want my kids to be aware of what is going on around them. They need to know about the struggles that our people and other people besides our race have endured so our children would have an equal opportunity to live in a nation that subjectively gives opportunities that normally aren't equal. Black children need to know that it was those struggles and sacrifices that were tools for change, not some law itself. They also need to know the other side of their heritage. They need to learn about other races and cultures. Black people and white people are not the only ones living in this world. And to add to that," she pointed to PT, "black children need to learn about the business culture and how to put back into their community and stop perpetuating the separation of rich and poor and light and dark.

"Too many of our black entrepreneurs are robbing the poor to give to the rich." Katherine expressed her thought openly. "Why would one group of people be so determined to separate itself from the other yet on the other hand be so willing to compromise their rules of segregation for economic gain?"

PT knew the comment was intended to attack his father and himself, but he first chose to address the issue of color as a means to an end. "Sometimes we have to use what we have to get us in the door and until there is some program or law that allows us equal entry, then we do what we have to do. And as for your other comment, I agree, Kat, such exploitation shouldn't be tolerated and that's why I plan on doing something about it."

"Spoken like a true politician, PT."

"What is that suppose to mean?"

"Show me before you tell me, that's what it means."

"Well, I can tell ya my father gives back and so will I."

Katherine's continued stance to unveil her legacy for her children was postponed upon the arrival of Seth. He stepped from around the side porch where he had been standing silently listening to much of Katherine's and his mother's argument. It was as if he couldn't escape the reality of his situation.

He put on his best smile when he saw Katherine sitting in the chair with legs crossed, cigarette in one hand, and tongue flapping away.

She jumped from the chair to her feet in a matter of seconds, wrapping both arms around Seth's neck, "There is my beautiful nephew."

"I thought I heard yo voice. Nobody told me you were comin'."

"You're leaving tomorrow, of course I was comin'."

"Is Aunt Nadine or any other kin folk comin'?"

"Ophelia," called Kat, then she suddenly turned to Claudia. "Claudia, did you call your aunties and uncles to remind them your brother is leaving?"

Ophelia shot out the starting blocks, "Why yes, and I spoke with Auntie Nadine and she said after she got off from the hospital she will be ova."

"Aunt Pauline and Aunt Monica didn't know, but I expect Uncle Joe and Uncle Tate are coming," Claudia added.

"Did you tell them there was going to be something to drink?"

"They asked and I said there would be."

"Then they'll be here. Seth, be sure to call your Uncle Gary in Richmond. Edna, do you have his new number?"

"He rarely calls me!" she said, with an after taste of bitterness.

"Well, I have his number and I'll make sure you get it, Seth, before I leave. Oh, your momma told me about your new girlfriend. You see, Edna, what you teach your kids to hate they end up liking. My Seth following in my footsteps."

The thought of her giving her kids away spurred Edna to impulsively leap with forceful words.

"I hope not."

"Hope all you want."

Katherine whispered in Seth's ear, "I'm proud of you for having a mind of your own. When I told my momma I wanted to marry a dark skinned man, she kicked me out and my daddy refused to speak to me. Seth, there are a few things in my life I regret doing, and one of them was allowing my family to talk me out of marrying my only true love."

"I thought you married him."

"Well, he wasn't my first love. Anyway, Seth, love is a wonderful thing and kids are a wonderful thing."

Seth had no idea where this confession birthed or its reason. Katherine was a strong woman and it was awkward for him to see her lose control over her emotions. She pulled back from him and wiped away the tears of misunderstanding.

"Are you crying, Auntie?" Ophelia questioned. "Momma, Seth said something to make Aunt Kat cry."

"No I didn't."

"The only thing that made yo Aunt Kat cry was that wine. Every time she drinks, she starts crying. She'll be all right."

"I'm ok," she confirmed. "So, Seth, where is this friend of yours, I can't wait to meet her."

"Hopefully she went home," blurted Claudia.

"Claudia, go find some logs to cut," scowled Seth, who had practically heard all he wanted to hear from Claudia in one day.

CHAPTER 9

9:02 p.m.
Saturday Evening

Edna would never accept what actually happened to the ten dollars as the truth, so Matilean and Victoria planned to fabricate a story that would relieve them of sure punishment. At the end of the alley, the girls rehearsed questions that Edna might ask.

"Remember, we was walkin' through the alley and a wino attacked us," Matilean said.

"A wino attacked us," Victoria repeated.

Matilean cloned Edna's voice, "How he attack y'all?"

"That was good Matilean, you sound just like Momma."

"Thanks, but answer the question."

"I don't know. How did he attack us?"

Matilean inhaled and filled her cheeks with hot air. No way was Victoria going to pull this off, she thought.

"We'll say he grabbed you around the waist and neck."

"Around the neck, ok."

"And waist, don't forget to say the waist. I kicked him to let you go, and we ran, but I dropped the money. Ok?"

"That won't work," a voice replied from within the dark of the alley. Little by little a thin man walked out from the shadow of the dark into the light. His disheveled appearance and odor of urine contaminated the air around him, making it unbearable to breathe. Victoria was familiar with the face. Surprisingly, she chose to heighten her tone to fabricate power over him.

"Why!" she gnawed.

"'Cause I know yo momma, and she ain't believing no cockamamie story like that—a wino attacked ya'll. Yeah, right." He ran his eyes over the contour of their bodies and laughed, "I'd rather have the wine."

"We gotta find that ten dollars," the girls said simultaneously.

"The only thing you gon find in dat alley is a bunch of old wine bottles and even older winos. Just go steal it," he suggested. "And when ya do, bring me back a bottle of Ripple."

That idea hadn't occurred to them, and from their position it was a pretty good idea. Victoria and Matilean headed back to the store.

"We can't steal wine," Victoria said.

"Think about what yo momma gon do to us if we ain't got that wine when we return. We already been gon a long time so we gotta come back with somethin'."

"You ever stole anything?"

Matilean sneered, "When I had to, and this is one of those times when I got to, but you gon help."

"What am I gon do?" she said nervously. "I never stole anything."

"You familiar with this store, right?"

"Yeah."

"Where is the wine kept?"

"It's kept in a corner near the front of the store where he can keep an eye on it. People always tryin' to steal from him, but he mean, down right mean. You know, he only got one leg so he liable to shoot us befo he chase us."

Matilean took the thought under quick consideration.

"Has he ever shot anybody?"

"He look like he has."

"What do that mean?"

"Like I said, he look like he has."

Matilean stored that thought in her mind.

"It's yo job to distract'im while I get the wine."

"How?"

"I don't know how, figure somethin' out and make sure you get the cracklin'. I can't get it all. Now you go in first then I'll come, and try not to look at me. I don't want him to think we together." Matilean remembered something, "Oh, when you sees me leavin' the store, come right behind me, ok? Don't be foolin' 'round, come right behind me."

A bell clinked to signal Do Drop of customers entering. An old crutch about two feet shorter than him supported his body. A half-smoked cigar was in one side of his jaw. Victoria put her head down and greeted his large bulging eyes with the side of her face. She spotted the cracklin, but also saw Do Drop's left hand hidden under a nearby newspaper. That was warning enough for her to abandon the mission, but Matilean had entered the store before she could retreat. Victoria played around the racks like musical chairs until Do Drop's scuffed voice yelled, "Ya want somin'?"

Both of their heads shot up, but Do Drop's eyes had settled in on Victoria. Not that it was planned, but it was enough distraction to allow Matilean to grab the wine.

"Huh?"

"I said ya buyin' somin'?"

Victoria had decided she wasn't sticking around any longer. She knocked over several of the racks and headed for the entrance door. Do Drop's eyes zeroed in on the fallen merchandise and the one rack that happened to be hiding Matilean came crashing down in front of her. She held both the bottles by their necks.

"What the...!"

Matilean saw something silver attached to Do Drop's hand when he pulled away from the counter. Wasting no time, she ran.

Do Drop and his one leg hopped from around the counter in chase. He took the crutch that supported his balance and slung it at the girls.

"Grab dem gals," he yelled.

"Duck," Victoria screamed, when a pair of hands reached out to grab Matilean.

Victoria followed Matilean and was practically out of the store when Matilean remembered the crackling.

"Don't forget the cracklin'," she yelled to Victoria.

Victoria had seen it on a rack just inside the front door, but the rack had fallen to the floor along with the other racks. She could see that the bag of crackling was still attached to the rack, so she reach down to grab it. In that moment Do Drop clamped Victoria's wrist with his silver hook.

Everyone at the storefront heard her screams, including Matilean. Victoria struggled to break his clutch and watched her only chance to escape slowly close. Maybe it was the struggle in her throat that made Matilean toss the wine bottles in a small patch of grass and run back. Do Drop was having his share of troubles pulling Victoria's half-free body back into the store.

The crowd of people hollered as he fought to balance himself and the cigar in his mouth. Matilean kicked the door open and stretched out to catch hold of Victoria's extended hand. As Do Drop attempted to seize her, he peered down over his nose and his teeth bore down on the cigar that was hanging from his mouth.

Bystanders inside and outside the store took the liberty to watch with roaring laughter. He began to curse them and then his cigar fell out of his mouth. The fire from the splattering ashes flashed in Matilean's eyes. Without releasing Victoria's hand, Matilean quickly lowered to one knee, grabbed the cigar off the floor, and rammed the burning end into Do Drop's leg. He couldn't hold Victoria and jump around and scream. The opportunity allowed Matilean to pull her through the door like a sling-shot. Their shoes could be heard hitting the surface of the street.

When in range of Victoria's house, only their heavy panting could be heard.

"All dat for some cracklin'?" Matilean huffed.

Victoria wheezed, "All dat so Mrs. Morgan can gnaw on them with her gums."

They laughed with difficulty.

"You din't tell me he only had one hand."

"I didn't know."

"He's a modern-day Captain Hook."

"I can't believe I stole something," she said with bewilderment.

"I can't believe I burned that man with his own cigar."

"I know, what came ova you?"

The question caught her by surprise, because she had always protected herself. But in this case, her heart had influenced her actions. She realized that she had accepted Victoria as a friend.

"We a team, ain't we?"

Victoria snatched her hand, "Sure we are!"

Pain immediately shot from Matilean's fingers up the length of her arm. How was it that pain always attached itself to wrongful acts? It never ceased to amaze Matilean that punishment always came and fit the sin accordingly.

"You ok?" asked Victoria.

"Yes, I'm ok," she said, while she massaged her hand. "I hit my hand on the door when we ran."

They walked towards the back of the yard. The guests had managed to sprawl around the entire house and in some dark hiding places. The girls displayed the latest hair fashions and wigs. They accessorized their looks with seamless, one-piece tights, and colorful shorts with short navel-revealing tops and wedge shoes, go-go boots, stiletto heel shoes, and hush puppies. The younger boys wore drainpipe trousers.

To Matilean, the crowd was exciting and vibrant, unlike the people at her mother's church gatherings. The church folks prayed, drank punch, and then talked about others who were either in church or not. At least here the hypocrites and heathens were upfront with each other.

CHAPTER 10

10:00 p.m.
Saturday Evening

Gradually the wine that had cloaked personal differences wore off, making it extremely difficult to maintain a peaceful atmosphere between the guests on the front porch—two guests in particular.

A brewing argument between Betsy Morgan and Katherine had ensued. Katherine lashed out with a deliberately sassy mouth in response to Betsy Morgan's continuous whispering.

"Betsy, what's so important that you got to keep whispering in Edna's ear? It really isn't nice to whisper about people while they are in your presence."

"Don't worry yo pretty self none 'cause I'll be sure to talk about ya wens ya gon too," she retorted.

Claudia pulled herself closer to the argument and smiled. She pleaded in mental telepathy that Katherine should smack the old lady in the mouth. Katherine understood defeat was guaranteed if she invited Edna to a brawl. So, she more willingly tried Betsy Morgan. As Katherine stood, Seth's long arms put distance between the two combatants. "Come on, Aunt Kat, Mrs. Morgan ain't talkin' 'bout you."

She nodded her head, "Yes she is, but all that envy and hate inside is going to explode one day."

The cigarette she smoked had burned down to a butt, but was still good for pointing at Betsy Morgan.

Betsy Morgan sighed, "Watch who ya pointin' at."

Katherine continued, "I know you been trying to hide your envy under all that fat you lugging around, even under that bad wig you wearing, and in between those big, funky thighs you're carrying around."

The cigarette butt identified the exact spots she referred to. "Every time you walk, mo friction builds and builds, and one day—pop goes the weasel."

PT and Ophelia buried their heads in each other's shoulder to conceal their laughter.

"Ah heas whatcha say, but my fat can still get up off dis heah sofa."

"Ain't nothing stopping you but those fat thunder thighs," blurted Katherine with inviting arms.

Claudia bounced from the far banister to her feet as if the invitation had been extended to her. She would have loved to challenge Betsy Morgan. She had more than a bone to pick with Betsy—mainly for all her allegations that got Claudia reprimanded and punished. She wanted a piece of her, and badly.

Betsy Morgan waved her hand towards Katherine and replied, "Gal, you really don't want me to get up from heah."

"You still talking? Get on up?"

Betsy Morgan gave a heavy rock to the back of the sofa and trampolined the momentum of her weight forward. She managed to climb to her feet.

"All right, don't you two start," pleaded Seth.

Of all people, Ophelia, the instigator of quarrels, nudged PT in the side to help Seth. PT knew that there was no way his thin body could hold Betsy Morgan back. When Ophelia gestured for him to go again, he quickly remembered Betsy Morgan hugging him so hard that she broke two of his ribs, so he told everyone.

Betsy Morgan called Katherine's bluff. Katherine hoped she could maintain her dignity in front of Edna. Continuously, Katherine scowled and threw her shoulders back like a charging bull, indicating her strong desire to fight to the death if need be. Edna shook her head and laughed while the two were being separated. Never before had she seen Katherine put on such a performance, and she knew it was all for her. She knew Katherine couldn't fight her way out of a wet paper bag; so instead, she awarded her with a soft ovation.

"Ok, Kat, you proved yoself, now come ova heah and sit down."

PT raced over and wrapped his arms around Betsy Morgan's body. She was a runaway locomotive full of steam, heading down an empty track. The moment Seth went to restrain Katherine, she eagerly sat down and shut up. The red glare in Betsy Morgan's eyes was a bit more than Katherine could chew—or wanted to chew.

Matilean and Victoria were unaware of what was happening on the porch. They thought the commotion was the sound of the party dancing all around them.

Eddie came charging out the screen door, carrying Biff.

"I told you I would find him, Seth! He was in the attic peeping through the ceiling cracks of the bathroom at the girls. Damn pervert. Sorry, Momma Edna."

Seth saw Eddie holding Biff, but was unaware of what he was saying. It was so noisy and chaotic on the porch, and when he thought it couldn't get any worse, it did.

"Come on, Seth!" demanded Eddie.

"What?"

"We need a stereo, man. How long you think PT's radio gon last? This crowd is getting bigger and bigger."

"Not long, because I don't want my battery to go dead," remarked PT.

Seth dared not enter the locked room without Edna's permission. She was the only one that could save him if his father found out who broke into the back room.

"All right, but don't meddle with his candy box. I don't wanna heah his mouth, and bring me a few of dem hoe cakes."

"But you just said..."

"Never mind what I said. I can get what I wanna get. I'm grown. Now go on befo I change my mind."

"Well, what about Mrs. Morgan and Aunt Kat?"

"Trust me, they're done."

Betsy Morgan scowled in Katherine's general direction before retaking her seat.

"Well, Momma, give me the key."

"Boy, yo daddy don't trust me with a key. Go through the window."

"I'm too big."

"Well, get Eddie to do it. He's skinny."

"I would," Eddie said shamefully, "but I'm scared of heights, Momma Edna. Biff can do it."

"Biff, go open the door fo'em."

Biff shook his head and jerked to get away from Eddie.

"You ain't going nowhere, so stop fighting. Now you heard Momma Edna."

"So. How much you paying?"

Edna smiled, "Give the boy some money."

Collectively they raised two dollars to persuade Biff to take the chance. He would have done it for free just because Biff liked adventure more than he liked money.

Eddie and Seth went along to make sure their investment paid off. Biff was known to run when you weren't looking.

Matilean temporarily slowed her pace before turning the corner; she wanted to be ready for what was about to happen.

"Wait, Matilean," said Victoria.

"What?"

"What about Momma's change? She gon want her change."

Matilean brooded over the question. Giving up, she replied, "Let's hope she don't ask."

Edna must have smelled the wine coming because she sat forward in her chair and sniffed the air like a hound dog. Her sudden distraction caused a few others in her general area to also point like hounds. Betsy Morgan finally shut off her faucet.

"I knew it had ta be som'um," raved Betsy Morgan when she saw the two bottles come around the corner. "'cause Edna ain't gon stop in de middle of a laugh if it ain't som'um extremely important."

The presence of alcohol calmed the out-of-control situation like a white flag waved in the midst of war. All the bad feelings and harsh words were forgiven as soon as they all took their first drink. It was as if the incident never took place, and once they got drunk the incident would never be remembered.

Disapproving eyes surged when Matilean and Victoria climbed the steps to the porch. They stood motionless in front of Edna, waiting for her lecture. Ophelia and Lillian burned on the inside. An extreme disgust curdled in their grunts and grimaces. It was bound to happen; fittingly, it was Lillian that coughed up her displeasure for Matilean's presence.

"Whatcha doin' on dis porch?"

Lillian's query wasn't the one Matilean had expected. Expected or not, she wasn't willing to answer. Lillian repeated the question again but this time with a harsher tone. Matilean focused on the wall behind Edna's head. An urge pressed her to look at Lillian and say something. The distinctive scent of hate was strong enough for Katherine to detect and bring to Edna's attention.

"I told her to come up heah." Edna sliced Lillian with a sharper tone.

"Why? Don't nobody like her."

"Hells fire, what I do in my back yard is my own business. Damn it to hell, I pay rent heah."

The argument belonged to Edna, but Claudia, who challenged every authority, would customarily come to Lillian's aid.

"But Daddy said for nobody to be ova heah."

Katherine turned Claudia's words back on her, "Well, who all these people? I must be seeing things."

"They different. They got permission."

Katherine's facial expressions revealed how she felt. Having this fight with her parents when she was growing up was enough; she was certain a young child wasn't going to make her endure the experience again.

"All she needed was permission? Hell, your momma gave her that."

She looked at Matilean, "You can be my guest, too." She looked back at Lillian, "Settled."

Katherine actually wanted to get up and shake the child, but she figured she would allow her authority to eat at her first.

Matilean searched her mind for a reason that made this stranger come to her aid.

"Sorry, Aunt Kat, you don't have authority to give someone permission to stay or leave. You don't live heah," hissed Claudia.

Now, she was itching to shake her. She even turned around to look at Edna for some support.

Then it registered with Matilean who this short, trim woman was—Seth's aunt Kat. Still, she couldn't help but wonder why Kat defended her. Edna acknowledged Katherine's frown for assistance and she gave Katherine just what she needed.

"I said she could be heah, now what? Be careful how you answer 'cause I'm 'bout to throw dis cup at you. And once dat hit you in the mouth, my shoe will be right behind it. Try me if you wanna."

Claudia knew if a word came out, the cup and the shoe would be on its way, so instead, she rolled her eyes and headed back to her previous corner. It was still pissing Katherine off that she couldn't shake her at least for a minute or two.

"I dos declare, so much tension," Ophelia spoke, while tossing her hair over her shoulder. "I see Matilean coming in as a big help." Matilean was so surprised that she nearly choked.

"She and Victoria can clean up after the party is over. I am sure there will be plenty of work available. I'm going to see where Aunt Pauline and Aunt Nadine are. They should have been here by now."

I know she ain't expecting me to clean up after them, Matilean thought. It killed her to smile with such a humble face. They didn't like her and she didn't particularly care for them. To clean up after them—that would be the day.

Edna surprised her, so did Seth's aunt, but at what cost, she couldn't help but wonder. It didn't take long for her to find out. Katherine looked out into the yard at a group of boys throwing phantom punches and arguing about who would win the upcoming fight between Muhammad Ali and Floyd Patterson.

"Look at them boys, will you?" directed Katherine with a subtle laugh. "They really think Cassius Clay, or Ali, or whatever his name is, is going to whip Floyd Patterson like he whipped Sonny Liston?"

Katherine had opened one of the topics of the day and many of the on-lookers eagerly added their comments and predictions.

"You don lost yo mind, Kat," PT laughed. "I guess you didn't see or heah about his fights against Sonny Liston?"

"I heard them both on the radio," replied Katherine, "and I still think Floyd gon win."

Ophelia laughed before adding, "Aunt Kat, you only rooting for that Floyd Patterson 'cause he black."

"We're all black baby, I like him because he dark black." She burst out laughing. "Now, I'd be wrong if I said y'all only like Cassius because he's light-skinned with a big mouth."

After Katherine made the comment, she looked over at Matilean. Matilean wondered if Katherine was implying that was her only reason for being with Seth.

Katherine had schemed a mental fight plan of words. Her fight was with Edna but she had to use Matilean. She had no intention of hurting Matilean—just Edna.

"Matilean, who do you think is going to win the fight?"

Matilean knew somewhere in the question was a hidden motive, and she really didn't want to entertain Katherine at her personal expense.

Matilean stalled for time, "Huh?"

All the spectators listened closely.

Katherine repeated the question elementarily so Matilean could answer the question, "Do you think Floyd Patterson is going to win or Cassius Clay?"

"I think Muhammad Ali is going to win."

"OOOOOhhh," initiated by spectators.

What Matilean knew about boxing, she learned from her brother and the neighborhood boys. She liked boxing. Truthfully, she liked Muhammad Ali for his looks, but she liked him more for his loud mouth antics and predictions of knockouts.

Immediately, Matilean thought about the neighborhood boys and how they desired to be Muhammad Ali: imitating his taunts, his flashy style of fighting, his facial expressions and his deadly anchor punch. Matilean wasn't brave enough to imitate Ali's style in front of everyone else, so she did it privately.

Katherine was going to milk the situation for all it was worth. She didn't care about hiding her intent, she wanted Edna to face the fact that her son was dating a darker woman and defying her wishes. That's what happens when you think you're better than someone else, Katherine contemplated.

"Muhammad Ali?" Katherine repeated and admitted, "he deserves to be called any name he wants."

She must have seen the first Sonny Liston fight because it appeared she wasn't going to fight fair. The subject of Ali changed to Seth.

Her first punch was a jab, "So, how long you and my nephew been dating?"

Matilean turned to Katherine and mulled over her question. She realized the only way to pay Katherine back for coming to her aid was to upset Edna. She wanted to believe that Katherine wanted to make her feel comfortable by discussing something she knew more about, which was Seth. However, Matilean knew better. Quickly, she dodged the jab, hoping Katherine would understand her position.

"We're just friends."

Katherine sympathized with her position but the answer wasn't good enough for what she wanted to prove to Edna, so Katherine threw a roundhouse punch with force.

"Friends? I thought it was more than that."

Was she better off to have Katherine delay the inevitable, and drill her in front of Seth's mother? Edna's blank facial expression was daring Matilean to give any answer other than the one she'd already given.

Matilean slipped the roundhouse punch.

"Nothing more."

Katherine had placed her in a feud that Matilean had no idea how to avoid. Sweat trickled down her forehead, and she wiped it quickly.

Katherine was frustrated; none of her questions were landing. The next question she threw was a hard left hook that was as potent as liniment; surprisingly the hook connected to Matilean's head. She tried hard to wipe out the sweat from her eyes. While Matilean's eyes burned and she searched for clarity, she had no answers for the assault of questions. Unfortunately, there was no Angelo Dundee to rinse her mind of chaos.

The spectators on the porch waited for Matilean's words; some hoped she'd say the wrong thing and go down in the round, while others hoped she'd survive to take the fight into further discussion.

Matilean's eyes and head cleared in time to duck Katherine's knock-out questions, "You plan on marrying him? Maybe have his kids?"

Matilean knew the consequences if she answered wrong. Within her, there was a burning desire to marry Seth. The questions had backed her up against the wooden rail. Fortunately, the wooden banister helped support Matilean's body, much like the ropes did for Ali. Matilean dug her short nails in the wood and rested momentarily to regain her composure.

Those with no stakes on the fight were surely entertained and those with stakes didn't want to lose what pride they had left. Betsy Morgan and Edna were so caught up that they had finished one bottle of wine and started on the other. Matilean pulled all their heads in closer when she smiled and came off the banister with her own combination—an invisible, quick, left jab, then a right.

"Sure, I wanna get married." Then something welled up inside of her, she paused, then confidently threw a damaging blow to Katherine and Edna's pride, "But why settle for Seth, I'm sure there's betta."

A crystal display of blankness gleamed from Katherine's pupils into Matilean's pupils. She and the entire porch crowd laughed. Some laughed at the absurdity of the comment, while others laughed in support of the comment. Regardless of their reaction, Matilean knew she had quality and wasn't going to allow any self-doubt to creep in. She wasn't going to lessen herself and appear desperate for any man. Even if she felt scared and desperate, they wouldn't know it. More importantly, she meant she was going to stand as strong as their tradition.

Katherine's reaction was evident that she had seen the second Ali and Liston fight. Matilean's answer didn't appear to hit Katherine's pride. If the question did make contact, surely it wasn't powerful enough to knock her out of the conversation. Yet, Katherine succumbed, either to save herself from further humiliation or to save Edna and Seth.

A moment later, Tate pulled up in his lumber truck filled with a bunch of lumberjacks that looked and smelled like they hadn't bathed in weeks. It wasn't so much Tate who distracted Katherine, but a dark, chiseled, picturesque physique in a half-buttoned shirt. Katherine thirstily watched as the men climbed off the back of the truck.

When the man's boots hit the surface of the pavement, his pectorals bounced like built-in springs.

"Ummm," murmured Katherine, "will you look at them muscles glisten all over his body. Look at the way his chest rises and flexes."

Betsy Morgan extended her neck to look over the banister. In the moonlight, the man's chest gave off a shining blue glair.

Betsy was quick to comment, "Listen like I tell ya, hea? It don't matta none if he got all dem muscles, 'cause I tell ya, if the right muscle don't rise, then he can say goodbye to me."

She and Edna gave a high five.

"They all look like they need a bath," announced Ophelia, as she scrunched her face upwards at all the men who bailed off the truck.

"No way," Katherine refuted, "he's just the way I like'em—rough."

"Tate done brought them poke woodcutters over heah again, Momma," observed Claudia.

"I can see."

Katherine walked to the front of the porch, caught in a temporary daze, "He sure can poke my wood."

"Who ain't don poked yo wood?" Betsy Morgan replied. "Wood been poked so much it should be dry rotted by now."

"You wish old lady," frowned Katherine. "Why don't you keep sitting in that rocker smelling like vinegar and pee, dry as a prune and rancid. I'm sure a buzzard will come by eventually and entertain you."

Claudia set back and laughed hard—hard enough for Betsy to notice. Katherine turned towards Claudia and asked, "Who is that dark-skinned man there?"

"Who? That boy?" Claudia corrected the statement.

"Naw, Claudia, no boy I ever known looks like that."

"Well, his name's Bigalow, he works with Uncle Tate. He's been 'round a couple of times."

Katherine pulled her head and attention back to the truck, "Why they call him that?"

"'Cause that's his name."

"Who in their right mind would name a child Bigalow? He appears short to me."

Seth walked to the banister and yelled down at the men.

Katherine scrutinized Bigalow and replied, "He really isn't that big."

"That's his nickname," Seth confessed. "And you don't have to be big to cut wood, Aunt Kat. You just gotta be strong and tough. Trust me when I say it, I worked with them guys and all of them are strong like an ox."

Amazingly, Katherine realized something and smiled gingerly.

"Bigalow," she repeated again before saying, "big- down-low."

Edna interrupted, "Daddy always said you was nastier than any of his sons."

Katherine smiled and patted around her bouffant hairstyle. "Well, I wouldn't want to disappoint him now. As dark as he is, why not call him Blue? But big-down-low has its advantages too."

Tate and his crew rushed the gate and up the steps. Matilean waited for him to offer some excuse or apology for why this very dark-skinned man was standing on Old Man Woodson's porch as though he belonged there. She waited for the hurricane to twist its way inland. Instead, Tate tilted his huge frame and scooped Katherine into his large arms like a rag doll. He pressed her fragile body into his old raggedy, smelly bibs. She let out an innocent scream and bashfully hugged him back while eye flittering with the men who watched.

"Boys," Tate said in a thunderous baritone voice. "Dis dea is my daby dister."

"You sure you ain't her father?" a man's voice screamed.

"Well, now dat Daddy's done, I'm dere, so I don't want da see none of d'all no-good-of-da cutting duttwipes 'round der."

Matilean tried to hide her laughter as she whispered to Victoria. "Why he talk that way? Did somebody tickle his feet when he was a baby?"

Victoria quietly explained, "Momma said he tongue tied. You know that thin piece of meat underneath your tongue?"

Matilean was confused, so Victoria tried showing her without everyone watching. She slyly opened her mouth, then lifted her tongue to the roof of her mouth.

"This piece here," she pointed at her frenulum.

"Oh, ok."

"Well, Momma said Uncle Tate's was stoppin' his tongue from comin' out his mouth. That's why it sounds like peanut butter is in his mouth. Momma said it sounds more like his tongue is attached to his bottom teeth. He has a hard time pronouncing certain letters. He puts the letter *d* in front of most of his words. If you remove the *d* you can pretty much keep up with what he's saying. When he gets excited, then I'm lost."

Matilean overlooked his speech impediment. She liked Tate's personality because he kept the entire crowd laughing. Tate was a gentle giant and he gently lowered Katherine to her feet only to pick up Edna and the chair she sat in.

"Go on, you ovagrown brute, smelling like oak."

She would complain while enjoying every minute of his kissing. He lowered the chair and respectfully nodded towards Betsy Morgan who tossed up her cup as acknowledgment, "Dell," he smiled, "dis dere any more of dat d'all drinkin'?"

"Huh?" wisped Betsy Morgan. "I can't understand ah word he sayin'. Sound like he's got a scoop of shit in his moufe."

Edna blurted, "Sure it is, an entire bottle." Then she revealed it from its secret hiding spot.

"Dell dell, don't be da stranger, dour me da dup."

Before plopping his tall frame and wide butt on the banister, he slowly turned to one of his men, "Little Bobbie, do to de druck and det me dat corn liquor under de deat. I keep it dunder my gloves, you dan't miss it, doy. Dit's dime to durn dis dea into a real darty."

Pitifully, Betsy Morgan shook her head and mumbled, "A real party? Is dat what he said? Shid, by time he finish a sentence, I'll be sleep."

Without moving from his comfortable spot, Tate reached out and grabbed Seth, placing him in a headlock. Seth's head disappeared behind Tate's large arm.

"Go on Uncle Tate, you always playin'. You don't know yo own strength. You liable to snap my neck by accident."

"Di'm liable to dnap yo neck anyway. Doy you didn't dven call me to let me know you was deaving."

"Somebody told you 'cause you heah."

"Yeah, my little drincess," he winked at Ophelia as he held a tight grip around Seth's head.

Matilean's eyes ran up and down Tate's huge frame. There was no doubt in her mind that he made Old Man Woodson look small, but without any dispute, Old Man Woodson made up for his size in meanness.

The arrival of the liquor allowed Seth to escape his uncle's massive grip.

"Go in the house and get some more cups," Edna ordered.

"Why?" asked Tate, "de all damily. What yo dreath won't kill de liquor will."

Half of the people understood and the other didn't care to understand.

"Please," cried Betsy Morgan, "somebody give his ass ah drink. Maybe if he get drunk enough, I might be able to understand'im."

Before Edna could reply Tate had turned the large jar up. He took several large gulps before he handed it over to Betsy Morgan.

"Deah."

"Dat I understand."

She wasted no time to turn it up to her lips. She gave a sour expression before passing it to Edna who quickly grabbed it.

Lillian tapped Edna on her shoulder, "Momma, you still want me to get them cups?"

"Nawl baby, we got it all under control."

CHAPTER 11

11:00 p.m.
Saturday Evening

Except for Seth, most on the porch laughed while the others waited patiently for their turn to suck from the jar. Seth watched with a mixture of pity and anger brewing in the pit of his belly. Edna's reckless drinking was slowly heating him to a boil. They passed the jar of corn liquor and wine around freely until it was gone. Tate quickly directed someone to run to his truck to get another jar. Seth could not take anymore; he took off into the house. Matilean wanted to rush after him but wisely resumed her position until the porch became claustrophobic. She and Victoria had somehow made their way to the steps. Matilean inspected both the yard and the porch.

For once she could sit and watch rather than be watched. Tate seemed to have a bottomless pit as he turned the second jar up and refused to let it down. Liquor spilled from his mouth to his chin; once finished, he was more than willing to lick the remainder up with his tongue.

Betsy Morgan and Edna were officially drunk. Betsy Morgan's wig lay lopsided on her head. When

Victoria pointed it out to her, Edna worked quickly to put it back in place. Unsuccessful at straightening the wig, Betsy Morgan and Edna playfully slapped each other on the cheek, then hugged. Suddenly, the old lady jumped, then screamed as her wig went sailing through the air. Hysterical, she knocked a few people out of her way, attempting to catch the wig before it went over the banister. It bounced out, then back into her hands. Edna laughed so hard that she fell from her seat. Still choking on laughter, she could barely get her words out, "What's wrong with you, Betsy? Did you see a ghost?"

"How in the hell she gon see a ghost when her eyes half closed?" a voice responded.

"Somin' bit me," she said, while inspecting the chair before sitting down. She brushed the seat with the wig, expecting to spot the insect and give it a taste of its own medicine. Under the wig, she wore an old stocking cap that was cut and tied at the ends. It kept her gray, matted hair tight so the wig would fit snugly.

Unashamed, she tossed the wig back on her head, quickly adjusted it, and then took her seat. "Whea is dat jug?" she huffed.

Matilean held her breath because Betsy Morgan's villain had mysteriously disappeared around the corner of the porch without being detected. Even though the porch was crowded, Matilean thought Betsy should have sensed Claudia's evil presence closely lurking around her. Yet, somehow Claudia had managed to slide around the corner of the house and take up position beside Betsy Morgan.

Matilean watched as Claudia jabbed the long knitting needle into Betsy's side. Upon the needle's return into Claudia's pocket and in the midst of all the excitement, its tip sparkled in the night. Matilean saw Claudia's eyes and the pleasure she got from delivering the blow.

Matilean twisted herself around to Victoria and opened her mouth to tell, but then she thought it'd be better to keep it to herself.

Victoria giggled, "That woman's paranoid."

Matilean chuckled with agreement, then placed her sights on something more exciting than Betsy Morgan.

Bigalow and Katherine had taken up in the far corner of the porch behind bystanders who laughed at Betsy Morgan's loud outburst.

Matilean ran a string of unanswered questions in her head. She watched as their skins consummated—a runny, brown hue. It was beautiful and unfolding right before her eyes. Matilean believed it was a sign. The sign of an unforeseen beauty that she knew existed even if only in a small corner of a crowded porch. It gave her hope. She smiled at their beauty. Katherine saw her watching and politely smiled before gripping the back of Bigalow's head and kissing him. She watched Matilean with one eye, making sure her message was well understood. Matilean didn't fully understand what Katherine meant; it might have been her way of bragging or daring her to try. In Matilean's heart she wished it were she and Seth in that corner. And the longer she watched the behavior of Katherine and Bigalow, the more their beauty faded. Nonetheless, she was still happy that someone was defying the rules of Old Man Woodson's household. As hard as she tried, she could not force her eyes to stop staring. Their faint laughter slipped in and out of the dark. Her scorn soon transformed into shear contempt for the two. She wished Old Man Woodson would suddenly appear just so she could see his reaction. He would surely throw Bigalow over the banister.

She looked around for Claudia or Ophelia. She wanted them to witness Katherine and Bigalow unchallenged by the same tradition that prevented her from ever being accepted. Watching them continued to tear at her insides. The scene was unbearable, it simultaneously created a pain and a faint hope that she knew was unreachable. She tried to look away, but found herself peeking at them again and again.

Bigalow pulled at Katherine's shoulders then plunged into the side of her neck. It wasn't until a passing car's headlights flashed on them did she push him away. Then Matilean knew it was all a show to plant a seed in her mind.

Curious to know if she was the only audience that they had, Matilean glanced around at the other uninterested faces. Katherine unkindly amused herself with Matilean's reactions. Bigalow was too dumb to know or even care that he was her puppet. Then again, maybe Matilean was the puppet. Conscious now that Katherine controlled all her actions and emotions, she felt it was silly of her to take the time to comb her hair, put on her Sunday outfit and best shoes just to be made a fool. Even the things that seemed good about this family spoiled over time. She buried the thought deep within, knowing her mind would wrestle with it later.

The noise of the crowd drowned the car's radio and the party needed an extra boost. Biff had changed his mind about sneaking into Old Man Woodson's private room to get the stereo. He hollered as Eddie squeezed his arms to force him to do it. "No!"

"But you promised you would!"

"So, I promise a lot of things. That don't mean I'm gon do it. Plus, it's tricky."

"What do you mean tricky?" glared Eddie.

Seth heard the commotion and entered the room. "I thought y'all would have gotten the stereo by now. What's taking so long?"

"Ask our little brother."

Biff sneered, "Ya mean his little brother. I ain't none of yo brotha. You always say that stuff as if it spose to get me to do somthin'. Who got you with that stuff?"

Seth interrupted, "Well, I'm asking you to do it. Ain't I yo Brotha?"

"Well, only Momma knows that. Momma's baby, Daddy's maybe."

Eddie burst into laughter, "He got you, Seth."

Biff couldn't restrain his laughter, "I did get'im didn't I?" Pointing, "You see his face?"

"You see my fist?" Seth was done with being nice.

Biff explaining, "I can't do it by myself, so y'all got to help."

"What we got to do?" retorted Seth. Still upset with Biff's sick sense of humor, Biff looked baffled at the moment. Then he smiled with a new discovery. "Well normally I'd get in from outside. I'd climb the old gutter along the house and then swing through the window. That was easy, but Daddy took down that old gutter."

"That old gutter?" questioning the story.

"Ain't no way, how you keep yourself up there?" Eddie asked.

"It was easy, but this heah is tricky," he admitted. "The girls' room is right ova de private room. I was thinkin' to do a backwards flip into his window, but the distance from their window to his window is too far for me to reach."

Biff smirked and said, "Eddie, the way I look at it, you tall enough, just the right length."

Eddie puffed out a few laughs, "Seth taller than me."

"But he's not small enough to get through Daddy's window; you are. You so skinny that yo ribs and stomach are fightin' for position."

"Biff, shut up," snapped Eddie.

"Even if I went, Eddie, I'm too heavy for you to hold my legs. From a side view, Eddie, you pretty much non-existent. There's no way I can fit through that window, but you sure can, said Seth."

"Nope, I ain't doing it!" he woofed.

"Well, it was yo idea to get the stereo," reminded Seth.

"I figger they can keep on listening to PT's radio. They ain't complaining none," said Eddie.

"Oh, it was ok for Biff to do it, but now that we need you, you don't want to help."

"It ain't that. What happens if I get stuck? How y'all gon get me out?"

"Through the do 'cause you ain't getting stuck. Trust me," Seth replied.

Eddie tried to stall the inevitable, shaking his head and even attempting to go back to the porch.

"Come on, Eddie, you my Brotha, ain't cha?"

"Ah damn, why you goin' there, Seth? You know I am."

"Well ack like it 'cause you wouldn't have to ask me twice. Hell, I wouldn't be wasting this precious air complaining 'bout it."

"Seth, I am scared of heights," cried Eddie.

"Time to ovacome that fear."

Seth had already started up the steps before Eddie could respond. Eddie knew he had to come through. For the first time, Biff was not repelled to be around the two; so far, he was more than eager to see the outcome. Biff followed at a close distance until they approached the room. With quick steps, he took liberty to raise the window, remembering to stick a tall block of wood between the window and the windowsill to keep it from crashing down.

Eddie's fear of heights was steadily making this an unattractive idea. His inner pride wanted him to be looked upon as a brother; that is what motivated him. He cautiously moved toward the window and peered from it. He dropped his eyes to look for the other window. When he didn't see the window, he retreated into the room and retracted all his promises.

"Seth, you my best friend, but you ain't to die fo."

Eddie's words caught Seth by surprise because he felt Matilean must be feeling the same way about the baby.

Seth felt he could help the situation. "Eddie, I'll be right here. I'll be holdin' yo feet." Finally Eddie reluctantly agreed to follow the plan.

"Don't let go!" snapped Eddie.

"I got you, Eddie."

"But are you sure you can hold me?" Eddie put most of his trust in Seth, and some portion of it in Biff's crazy idea. "Ok, but don't expect me to do a backward flip."

"Ah, I was only messin' wit ya, Eddie," Biff declared.

Eddie took another look out the window. "That's a long way down." He slowly leaned out the window. His eyes hunted through the threatening darkness, which hid the window beneath him. He tilted forward then began his slow descent. He crawled until his body was completely flat and until his arms were completely extended. Still, the outline of the window wasn't felt. He yelled back, "I don't feel it."

"What?"

"I said I don't feel it." Eddie's eyes widened when Seth insisted on letting him down a little more. Eddie strained his eyes to see the edge of the window. "I see it, I'm almost there."

Seth gripped both ankles tight against his chest. "Hurry up, you getting heavy."

This wasn't so bad, Eddie thought, until Seth lost his grip around one of his ankles. Eddie felt his body slip. He screamed. As his body fell a few inches below the window, he felt as if his heart had dropped into his throat. Seth managed to clutch his pants leg, stopping Eddie's freefall. Biff laughed quietly.

"Stop that laughin' Biff and help me!" Biff reached out and took hold of Eddie's other flailing leg.

"We got you, so hurry up."

Eddie dug his fingernails between the crack of the windowsill. He kept digging, though his nails bled. The window finally gave and jarred slightly upward. He managed to lift it half way to flip his body in.

Once inside the room, Eddie buckled and then the window gave way.

"Wham!"

He took slow and deep inhalations of air, pulled himself to his knees, and used his shirt to wipe the perspiration from his face. Eddie, unlike Seth, had managed to face his fears. He stayed on his knees a few more minutes before brandishing a wide smile of accomplishment. Eddie then moved stealthily through the room in search of the lamp.

"Eddie!" called Seth. Moments passed without an answer. The light clicked on and Eddie lifted the window to peer out. It wasn't until he peered down that he saw the gutter running up along the house perfectly intact.

"Biff!" he screamed, "I'm going to kick yo butt."

"Uh oh." Biff fled.

"Eddie," Seth peered down at him.

Eddie was livid. "The damn gutter is right here; that boy lied just so he wouldn't have to do it. And you knew I was scared of heights, Seth."

"You not scared of heights anymore." Seth turned to berate Biff and realized he had vanished.

"Well, open the door 'cause he gon."

"He better be gon 'cause when I catch up with him I'm gon pluck his nose hairs out. I risked my life for a darn stereo. And I want my money back fo doing it."

"Well what's the difference between you and him?"

"I'll tell ya the difference, he like doing crazy stuff."

"Go on and open the do, I'm comin' down."

The lamp partially lit the family room, but that made no difference, Seth knew exactly where Old Man Woodson had hidden the snacks. He rushed over to the back portion of the room, slid to both knees, and pulled at the lock on the nineteenth century hand carved trunk. The lock had a removable front that was anchor shaped with a beautiful geometric design. He drew his hunting knife and tweaked the tip of the blade into the small opening of the lock until it popped. It was a treasure chest filled with loose dollar bills, cakes, candy, liquor, and beer.

"Will you look at all that money?" Eddie said shockingly, while holding his hand out. "Hand me a couple of those dollars. I'm sure yo daddy won't miss'em."

Seth slapped at Eddie's reaching hand. "See, you would be the first to die in a real treasure hunt. You neva watched a pirate movie? The pirate always set somethin' right in front of you to entice you to grab it. Then, gotcha, you dead."

"Right!" Eddie smirked in disbelief. "Well, at least let me take back my dollar that I gave to Biff."

"Take that money and you'll see. Just get the snacks and the beer, but not all ov'em."

It took less than two minutes to ransack the old chest for half its treasures.

Quickly Seth stretched out his arm and slid open one of the doors to the 1960 Victrola stereo that his father had recently purchased. Old Man Woodson threatened to destroy anyone who laid a finger on it. Seth's guilty face reflected in the gorgeous finish on the stereo. A golden trim outlined the edges. The stereo was not like a valued treasure but rather was stuffed in a space underneath the two-knobbed radio.

Seth tossed the Victrola stereo cord over top the stereo and wheeled it onto the porch.

"Get the extension cord from the kitchen," Seth ordered.

"Seth, can we take the television? I want to watch Dick Clark's 'American Band Stand'."

"Naw, plus you already missed it."

Immediately the crowd parted at the sight of the stereo, it had the same effect as the staff that Moses used to part the Red Sea. Eddie threaded the cord through the den window and then paused to look at the equipment. A furtive grin sketched across his face before he flipped the switch. A green light illuminated the darkness that had swallowed up much of the porch. It took a few seconds before electro metallic sound waves emitted from the speakers; the first utterances resembled two pieces of sand paper being rubbed together. He twisted the knobs for a station. The crowd waited impatiently, hurling a few snide remarks. Then a scratchy voice came from the speakers, "This is WDAO-Night Train bringing you the old and the new hits, so help me." Before the disk jockey could supply the crowd with a song, the radio went out. Seth blinked, trying hard not to show signs of panic.

He turned to Eddie. "Eddie, did you get the records?"

"They should be in the side compartment."

Seth pulled the compartment back and underneath a dirty cloth was a line of records.

Eddie looked over to Seth, "Seth, them records look old." He reached for one, "I don't even know who this is."

Seth wiped the dust from one of the records.

"Who's that?" asked Eddie.

"It says Fats Domino."

"That sounds old."

Seth corrected, "It's not a that, it's a man, stupid."

"Well, he sounds old. He got any newer records?"

Seth flipped through various records until he came to James Brown. "You can't go wrong with James Brown."

Eddie took the record from Seth to get a better look at its condition. "Hey, this new."

"You got some records at yo house?" asked Seth.

"Yeah."

"Go get'em while I set everything up."

After Seth cleaned off the stereo, he calmly put on the first record. The first record had already been decided—James Brown's, "Papa's Gotta Brand New Bag." A horn-driven shuffle accompanied James Brown's cool and raspy voice.

Immediately, Edna struggled from her chair and jerked Tate's hand. "Come on, Tate."

Like newlyweds, they took the first dance while on lookers laughed with the pleasure of seeing the old timers strut their stuff.

"Don't hurt'em, Edna!" Betsy Morgan screamed; then she took a quick sip before screaming again, egging on her good friend.

The boys held their imitation guitars and pretended to be Jimmy Nolen when Jimmy riffed the "ting-a-ling-aling-aling part of the song."

"Can I put it on him?" Edna asked with a serious facial expression. "Put it on him!" the crowd rose in laughter. Edna slowly sank to the porch but called for immediate assistance in lifting herself.

"My knees ain't what they used to be," she commented.

It was her way of sitting down for another drink. In a matter of seconds the entire outdoor party was doing the twist, the jitterbug, the jerk, the mashed potato, and the stomp.

Matilean squirmed in her seat and occasionally tossed her hands up. She loved to dance. At every opportunity, she would dance, even when no music accompanied her body's motions.

"That's my song, girl," said Victoria, who was as stiff as a plank rendering a simple two-step.

"Mine too," replied Matilean.

The wood beams vibrated along with the beat of the music. Seth maintained the crowd's merriment with the Supremes' "Stop! In The Name Of Love." Edna called Ophelia, Lillian, and Victoria to the center of the porch to do their rendition of the Supremes' choreography. Before any of the other girls could claim the role of Diana Ross, Ophelia seized it for herself.

Eddie had returned with a number of hit songs.

The crowd danced; the more they danced, the more they drank. They drank heavily, knowing they had nowhere to go the next day. The scene suddenly shifted when the long, tall red-wood-of-a-man came crashing down. "Timber!" a voice screamed. Tate hit the porch with a thunderous pound and a backlash of dust from his clothes mushroomed into the atmosphere. He lay drunk and unconscious, stiff as the logs he cut and just as heavy to move.

"Aw, damn, he don passed out," Edna growled. Then she fanned her hand towards several of the men standing around watching. "Ten of you boys pick'im up and take'im 'round the side of the porch."

The first attempt to move him was unsuccessful, so another ten boys joined to help move Tate's body to the sofa on the side of the porch. Seth quickly put on another record. He played the prelude of the next song. The beat pulsated in their ears. Before the artist could say a verse, a voice walked into the yard singing it for Otis Redding. Pauline's singing enticed the crowd to join in. They all mimicked the words exactly.

Pauline stopped temporarily at the steps; rather, the buzz from the music stopped her at the bottom of the red steps. Nadine, a ruddy-face, quiet type, pushed her sister Pauline into the smoke and drink filled environment.

Thick-necked guys and girls wearing tiny shorts with pigtails and barrettes in their hair filled the porch, the steps, and the yard. Matilean ignored the various eyes, which resented her being there. She became more comfortable with her surroundings, allowing herself to feel the music and letting her head bounce to its beat. She shouted over the din of music to Victoria, "Do you see Seth?" She wanted to dance. Minutes later she was pulled from her seat by an inebriated, short, stout, bare-chested fellow. He grabbed her by the waist and rubbed his hands over her skirt.

The horde of people shimmied together. Matilean tried not to dance too close. She disliked the guy's bad breath and refuted close contact by offering him a hideous face. Unexpectantly, the shoulders of the intoxicated boy were abruptly pulled back and slung down the stairs. He turned quickly to charge back up the steps. Then he saw who the initiator was. Matilean's smile showed her gratefulness upon seeing Seth's appearance. Sweet gravity couldn't have pulled Seth closer. The intoxicated boy saw the seriousness in Seth's eyes. He chose not to go into battle. He retreated down the stairs and disappeared in the massive crowd of young people.

Matilean and Seth looked around at the crowd of people and moved to blend in with them. Though they hadn't seen each other all night, the emotional connection between them had somehow been retained and Seth acknowledged it.

Claudia bullied her way to the front of the porch; her jaw dropped when she saw Matilean and Seth cuddled. She watched vengefully as they danced. Just seeing Seth's arms around Matilean sowed additional hate in Claudia while assuring Matilean solace and safety in an atmosphere cultivated by old tradition and hate.

She could have spent forever mired in this moment in space and time. That moment gave her a state of euphoria in her heart, giving her back a glimpse of hope that had all but disappeared. She looked into Seth's eyes, hoping to see the same emotion. Matilean wanted to catch the layers of his previous implacable decision being peeled away.

Meanwhile, Claudia had masterfully concealed a plan to persuade, better yet to force, Matilean from their house. It was tearing out her insides to stand there and see Matilean act as if she were part of their family. Claudia grunted, "Look at her black butt hugged up." She waved for Lillian to join her.

"What in the world?" Lillian paused, "Seth don lost his mind. He don forgot where he is."

Lillian's eyes stared at their pressed cheeks and their laced fingers. She turned back to Claudia. "So whatcha got in mind?"

"I can show you betta than I can tell ya." She offered an evil smile.

"You know Daddy won't mind a bit if we got rid of her. He already told her he don want her comin' 'round heah. I got a good mind to go down there and pull her hair right out by the roots," replied Lillian, after remembering what Matilean had done to her earlier.

"No, you wait. There is plenty of time fo that. Let her keep gettin' comfortable. Let her feel like she's at home."

Lillian smiled, "You ruthless, Claudia."

"I know."

"Do you want Ophelia to know?"

The cruel girl threw her head over her shoulder towards Ophelia's direction and remarked, "Why? She ain't 'bout to do nothin'; it'll be a waste of her time and a waste of my energy to ask. Betta she stayed bear-hugged like she is. Plus, PT would come lookin' fo her and end up ruining my plans."

Claudia's thoughts lurked in the cruelest part of her mind. She had a demonic face that showed evil was present. Claudia stared at Seth and Matilean enough for Pauline to notice in passing. Pauline asked Claudia what was so disturbing that her eyes and nose fought her lips and cheeks. Before Claudia could look away, Pauline caught the blazing path to Seth and Matilean.

"Well, it looks as if your Brotha has taken a page out of Kat's book. Times are a-changing, baby."

Claudia grunted. Pauline's words meant nothing to her. "Why do it have to change?" The tone in her words increased with each syllable.

"That's just the way it is, but before you burn a hole in the two of them why don't you go and get me a drink?"

Pauline peered back down at the two and smiled gingerly when Seth looked up and waved.

"Who's that, Seth?" Matilean asked, as his eyes turned back to hers.

"That's my Auntie Pauline."

"She's beautiful. She looks white."

"And she knows it. She musta come directly from work. She still in her uniform."

"Yo family always come out for things like this?"

"As long as I can remember."

The remarks passed through her ears easily. She fell into his chest and gripped his shoulders from underneath his armpits. Everything was happening so fast, things that she would have never imagined. She delighted in the thoughts. She believed that now Seth wouldn't keep pushing for the trip to West Virginia. It was possible that his family was willing to accept her. The change may be difficult at first, but they would come around to their having the baby, maybe even getting married, so she hoped.

She could remember that once her mother laid eyes on Ruth's baby, it wasn't long before she started visiting. She was sure, more than sure, it would all unfold happily much like the ending of a picture show. Surely God wouldn't let her have anything but a happy ending, she thought; then again, maybe unhappiness was her punishment.

Her mother had always said that God had his way of working it all out. In her mind, she concluded that God was doing exactly that. His actions spoke loudly through her mother's words. With Matilean's faith wavering, she wondered if God would be enough.

The thoughts came one after the other, cluttering her mind until she closed her eyes and tried not to think at all. For the moment, she loved the touch of Seth's thick body against hers. Through all Seth's indecisiveness, she loved him still, hoping that he felt the same. This was the love she found underneath the staircase that somehow went astray. Her stomach stirred like a colony of ants on crumbs, so she tugged at his shoulders to reassure herself. She considered the thought again while her face rotated from one side of his chest to the other.

He didn't know what to feel. Matilean would have seen that if she looked past the glare in his eyes. How did it all come to this, he thought? He knew the literal answer to that question. What he really wanted to know was what possible way could he break this to his father and make it all right. There was a time when he would have never stood up to him, yet he found himself doing that very thing earlier. He raised his head proudly in partial accomplishment. I can do it again, he considered. Seth realized he was building himself up just to face his father, but he wasn't sure if he would survive a second encounter. His chances of returning from Vietnam were greater than his chance of recovery after telling his father that Matilean was pregnant. Abruptly, all his courage melted away. He pulled away, angry with himself for not being man enough to try.

"What's wrong?"

"It's nothing. I gotta change the record befo they get upset."

Holding her hand, he led her back to the stoop. "Sit with Victoria until I come back."

She sat down, clinging now more than ever before to each of his promises.

Excited, Eddie pulled the next record.

"Seth, go on and dance, I got this. I saw you ova there cuddled up."

"Darn!" Seth smacked his forehead. "I'll be back. Can you handle the stereo?"

"Relax, Seth. Remember this is yo night, yo party, so enjoy it. By the way, did you see Sabrina?"

Eddie pointed her out in the crowd of people.

"She's ova there with Claudia, and she's looking good, too. I'm not the smartest guy, but I'd give five dollars just to smell her armpits—two fifty for each pit."

"Eddie, don't eva repeat that again, to no one. Better you just play the records, and I'll be back befo you know it. Who's that girl with Sabrina? She keeps looking at you."

"That's Cinnamon."

"Looks like Cinnamon got the sweets for you," smiled Seth.

"I got a good feelin' that girl from yo last party is gon show up."

Eddie nodded, then put on the next record, a slow song by the Temptations, "My Girl." Matilean's eyes searched for Seth. She wanted to dance with him. Striving for Seth's attention, Sabrina went well out of her way to grab his arm just as he reached for the screen door.

Matilean carefully observed the way Sabrina's hand slid from Seth's elbow down to rest in the palm of his hand. No she didn't, she thought.

"Mr. Man, where are you going?"

"Sabrina! Where did you come from?"

"I just arrived a few minutes ago." She glanced around, clutching his hand.

Sabrina was plain to look at. Her makeup began to chip like old paint, but it didn't stop Matilean from keeping her in focus. Seth knew that if Sabrina dared to follow him in the house all hell would break loose. Matilean stared at Seth with a look of apprehension in her eyes, as if she evaluated his resolve against hers.

Victoria was watching just as intently as Matilean. "I wonder what she wants with Seth."

"I got a good idea, but not while I'm heah," said Matilean.

"Huh?"

She moved her mouth without turning her eyes, "It's only an expression."

Sabrina pushed up closer, her breasts brushing against his shirt. His tongue glazed over his jovial lips, his eyes tilted towards her cleavage. She went so far as to whisper in his ear. Seth struggled to control himself; he did his best to keep his expression uninterested.

Matilean kept Sabrina under close surveillance, "Look how she's throwin' herself on him."

Eventually Seth satisfied Matilean's inner fears by stepping back from Sabrina and entering the house alone.

Matilean sighed with relief, "I don't want to start trouble, but there was gon be some trouble if she stepped in that house."

Sabrina walked back in Claudia's general direction. Claudia began to feel the urgent beat of time pressing in on her plan, so she hatefully side-nodded to signal Sabrina to go after Seth. She had a gut feeling that if Matilean cared anything about her brother, she would give chase.

That's exactly what happened when Victoria brought it to her attention. "Sabrina just went into the house."

Matilean uttered a soft whisper and grabbed Victoria by the arm. "I need fo you to get me in the house."

Victoria noticed that Edna was too close to the door; she would spot them if they tried entering from the front, so instead, she escorted Matilean around to the back.

"Come with me," directed Victoria.

Once at the back of the house, they had trouble getting in through the back door. Victoria momentarily paused from pushing the door. She searched through her mental Rolodex for an alternative route into the house.

"Can you cook?" she asked.

"Yes, but why?"

"You sure?"

With Victoria leading, they trotted back to the front of the house. Claudia was surprised to see them; she figured they would have had no problems getting in through the back. When they approached the steps once more, the pace had slowed to a creep. Victoria stepped onto the porch, followed by Matilean.

Matilean didn't care what Victoria's plan was for getting her into the house as long as she got in.

When Edna saw the girls approaching she sat up like a slow explosive. In slow motion, both of Edna's eyes slid into a soft collision. Her head slowly fell back to her shoulder. The liquor penetrated her tongue, numbing it; when she talked, she spat and mumbled.

"What is it?"

"I was wondering if you wanted something to eat?"

Claudia pulled close to eavesdrop on the conversation. Edna's mind conjured up a list of things she wanted fixed, and then she twisted around in her chair. "Who's cookin'?" Before an answer could be given, she asked, "Where is Claudia?"

The moment Claudia heard her name called her body had surprisingly vanished. "'Sides my own, I don't trust anyone else's cookin' except Claudia's."

"I haven't seen her," acknowledged Victoria.

Matilean had an urgency to say something. "Mrs. Woodson, I can cook."

"Cook what?"

"Practically anything."

The chugging of her throat, the slapping of her tongue against her lips, and the weight of her eyelids made it evident that she was about to pass out. She would have if Victoria had not tapped her on the shoulder. Her head whipped to the rear, followed by her tongue, which rolled to the right of her mouth.

"Whatcha say, Betsy?"

Edna wasn't aware that her friend had passed out, leaving her mouth and legs sprawled open. Although Matilean lost time, she knew there was no way she could proceed into that house without Edna's consent. That consent was all that was missing and it seemed like forever passed before Edna dismissively waved her hand at the two of them.

"So you want something to eat?" Victoria asked again.

"Go'n and make me some beef stew, and don't put no sugar in it."

Before Edna's head returned to its hung position, the girls were in the house. Victoria went scampering through the foyer, but Matilean stopped and looked in awe at the gold chandelier that hung from a high Victorian ceiling. A marvelously tulipped motif was deeply carved into the wooden border that enclosed the entire ceiling. She hadn't seen anything like it. Her eyes followed the border all the way around the room to the light blue painted walls that remained untouched by cobwebs, loose dirt, or fingerprints. An exquisite wood-grain staircase lined the far right wall.

Matilean spotted her dark complexion in a very beautiful and ornate mirror, carved with floral designs and a braided trim around parts of the frame. Straight ahead of her was a mahogany desk with a black rotary dial telephone and a black, gooseneck desk lamp. Though beauty was all around her, the picture over the desk drew her attention. An egg-shaped frame held the box-structured chiseled face.

Matilean could hardly believe that Old Man Woodson was once young. She walked up to the picture and considered it and Seth's similarities. One would be fooled if not taking the time to look closer. She stepped backwards. To the left of the foyer was a sliding door to the dining room. Curiously, she pulled the doors apart and peeped through. Sneaking a peep blossomed into stepping into the charming burgundy room. She hated to even walk in the room, afraid to disturb the stillness that lived there. Yet, she couldn't resist.

The striking room housed a dining room table that occupied much of the room with its double pedestal ball and claw legs, and hand-carved roped edges. The table accommodated ten pierced chairs with vase-shaped vertical slats and drop-in seat cushions that were upholstered in a beautiful white brocade fabric to coordinate with the burgundy interior of the room. A giant chandelier, larger than the one in the foyer, with a shine like that of the sun, hung low over the center of the table. A china cabinet with a mirrored back and beveled glass on the sides displayed all the dishes. A fine looking fireplace and mantel full of family pictures and a long heavy side-board that looked very old, but sturdy, also furnished the room. All the items were custom made from solid mahogany.

As Matilean wandered around the room she was amazed at how beautifully it was accessorized. She could not find a nick or a scratch on any of the furniture. She spotted one of Seth's pictures on the mantel. A younger smile filled with teeth appeared as innocent as underneath the staircase. The entire room was stunning, simply stunning.

Her survey of the room took only a few minutes. She continued to wander freely until she came to another sliding door. Hesitating, she carefully pulled the doors slightly back. Through the crack she could see another room. This must be the living room, she thought. She pressed closer to the crack. The gold from a large French gilded mirror brightened a large portion of the room, and she saw the heavily carved, skirted base and cabriole style legs of the mahogany French Victorian sofa.

Her eyes scrolled up the legs of the sofa, admiring the wonderful floral carvings and carved center design. Her sights crossed over to the chair. The design was the same as the sofa. While Matilean's eyes quickly circled the room, inspecting additional detail, she heard her name being called.

"Matilean!" Victoria whispered loudly from the edge of the foyer and the dining room. She was more than careful not to cross the line. "Girl, Daddy would kill you and me if he knew we was in this room. Come on out befo Claudia or Lilly see you."

Matilean had forgotten to close the sliding door from the dining room to the living room, but Victoria was cautious in sliding the door closed from the dining room to the foyer.

"I didn't know where you went off to."

Matilean recalled the purpose for being in the house.

"I thought you wanted to find Seth."

"Oh, I do, but yo house is so…."

"Never mind that. I looked in the kitchen and the back rooms, but I didn't see any of them. Come on, let's go upstairs."

"You think it's ok? I mean yo mother might wake up and…."

With a confident smile Victoria replied, "She not waking up til mornin'."

They skipped every other step to make their journey up the stairs quicker. The upstairs lacked the immaculate beauty that was found downstairs. To their immediate left were two rooms with their doors open. In front of them was a long, narrow, and what seemed to Matilean, endless hallway that curved at the end, cutting off any illumination from a swinging light. The partially lit hallway was dark and ghostly.

"I hate comin' up heah, even in the day time; I hate comin' up heah," complained Victoria.

Matilean could empathize because her cold basement gave her the same chilling feeling.

"Somebody is up heah," stated Victoria.

"How can you be fo certain?"

"'cause the light wouldn't swing so fast."

"You think it's Seth?"

"I hope. This is an old scary house. At night when I'm sleepin', I hea voices comin' from the attic. Momma says she heas them too, but she stays so drunk, she probably hea herself talking to herself."

"All right, Victoria, if you're tryin' to scare me you did—so stop."

Matilean could hardly breathe, and horror filled her eyes, keeping alive her fears. The long and scary hallway had taken her courage and forced thoughts of turning back into her mind. Suddenly, Victoria fell into a terrified paralysis that prevented any forward movement.

For some strange reason, the hall was more frightening that night than ever before. Victoria could sense the presence of evil lurking from its hidden corner, waiting to jump out and attack them. She invited Matilean to proceed and Matilean coerced herself to comply. She forced herself to think of it as only a hallway, nothing to be frightened of; the menace was only a swinging shadow. It would only take a minute or two to walk the entire hall, she thought.

Matilean began to sense a feeling of uncertainty in her steps. If something were going to get me, it would have gotten me by now, she thought. She came upon the first bedroom. She barely touched the doorknob before it swung open. Her head whisked back for Victoria. Victoria had not moved a step. In case anything happened, the stairs were close enough for her to make an escape. She never considered what might happen to Matilean.

Matilean peeped into the dim room. Seeing no sign of life was her excuse to close the door and continue on. The hallway grew lighter the closer she walked to the hanging cord; it offered her a small safety net. Standing near the light, at least she would have time to see something coming before it snuck up on her.

Matilean spotted another door just out of the rim of the light. The tension had heated her sweat glands and perspiration ran into her eyes. She inspected the room and noticed it too was mute and lifeless. She soon came near the end of the hall, well out of the light. Victoria still saw the red in her blouse and used it as a guide to identify her positioning. Victoria called to her, "Come on back Matilean, he's not up heah."

Victoria could no longer see her, but she could hear her voice in the darkness.

"I got one room left to check," her voice echoed from the dark, curved hallway.

She wanted to be sure Seth and Sabrina weren't hiding in one of the rooms because she was certain she wasn't returning. Her small hand trembled as she turned the knob and pushed the heavy door inward. The door whined and moaned as she opened it. Matilean gathered her courage and prepared one fist just in case something stormed her way.

CHAPTER 12

12:00 Midnight

The moon's transient rays streaming through two windows in the room provided more than enough light to see a large portion of the room. The light enticed Matilean to enter the room but she didn't unravel her fist. She kept her fist near her chin and cocked. Victoria could see just a line of light through the door, and it disappeared as the door closed behind Matilean.

Matilean hoped it all wasn't a sick game Seth was playing. He loved playing games, and he knew she hated being scared just as much as she hated spiders—and she really hated spiders. The door closed hard. Matilean jerked and slowly moved with both fists in the air.

She called several times for Seth, but there was no answer.

"Whooo, it's nothing," she waved.

There was a closet in the room and she noticed the door was closed. Her insecurities of not knowing whether Seth and Sabrina were in the closet moved her closer towards the door. Passing clouds momentarily blanketed the moon's rays, and the room fell pitch dark. She heard her own heart beating. She could barely see in front of her. Her complexion camouflaged her in the dark of the room. They blended perfectly without anyone ever realizing she was there.

Victoria was afraid, too; she hadn't heard a sound and Matilean refused to respond to any of her calls.

"Matilean come on back," she called again, "please come on back."

The light began to flicker on and off. Victoria grabbed the wooden ball on the end of the banister and felt with her foot for a step. The fear inside of her began to bubble and boil; she wanted to run.

Matilean considered waiting for the light of the moon before attempting to open the closet door. Suddenly, ill feelings overcame her; maybe it was better to walk blindly back to the door than staying another second in that room. She yielded; forget it, it's only a closet, she thought. This time, she figured, she would trust Seth.

Behind her, something moved from the corner. Her head whipped in the direction of the noise, instinctively her fists locked in fighting position. From the opposite corner she heard shuffling feet. The closet door rushed open, smacking her in the back, and caused her to fall to the floor. Swiftly she jumped to her feet, closed her eyes, and swung hard through the air, connecting. The body could be heard crashing into the wall, then crumbling to the floor. A sharp pain pierced Matilean's hand after she threw the punch. Like a chameleon, she adapted to the situation. She used the darkness to camouflage herself. She squinted her eyes, stepped back, squatted, and waited for the shuffling feet to approach her.

"Where is she?" a voice whispered.

"I don't know, I can't see her," another voice answered.

Smeared against the darkness was this yellowish haze. The moment the haze approached, Matilean stood and punched straight out with her good fist. The figure screamed and drifted to the right. Matilean followed the blow with another punch. The force of the blow drove the yellowish hue into the glass window. Glass shattered. Again Matilean grimaced from the pain in her hand.

As soon as Matilean realized they could not see her without the light of the moon, she prayed the cloud took its time to pass, at least enough time for her to reach the door.

Matilean stole a peep out the window. Only the tail of the cloud was left to drift across the face of the moon. She knew the full radiance of the moon would shatter the darkness in the room, exposing her to whoever was there. Matilean didn't want to be detected, so at a snail's pace, she crawled towards what she assumed was the door.

She didn't want to believe that Victoria had set her up to meet with calamity. They were friends, she believed. Matilean felt more distance from this family on the floor than ever before at that gate.

She felt the presence of the door. She was certain it was the door because she felt a breeze coming from somewhere and as low as she was, it must have been coming from the hallway, seeping under the crack of the door.

Matilean was unaware that the tail of the cloud was gradually exposing the moon, and the light of the moon was steadily erasing the darkness in its path. The moon's light flowed over a few boxes on the floor, over the body of Sabrina, who was out cold, over Lillian and shattered glass, and over the dusty floor panels before jumping to her head, then to the door and ghostly moving upward toward the ceiling.

Her head was jerked back. The pain from her hair being yanked out of its roots and her body being snatched to its feet shot through her body. A force coiled like a snake around Matilean's neck and suspended her in the air, choking her. The strangler's hot breath panted over the back of her neck. She tried to break loose but whoever was lynching her was strong. This can't be happening, she thought. The tips of her shoes tapped for the surface of the floor. Matilean's arms swung violently through the air while her eyes bulged.

She now knew what it felt like not to be able to breathe. Her struggle for freedom didn't seem to be having an effect on her assailant. Luckily, Matilean was able to drive the heel of her shoe into the top of the assailant's foot. Her effort to gain freedom was a success. The assailant huddled over and let out a long grunt, either from the staggering pain from the blow to the foot or from anger brewing within.

Regardless, Matilean seized the opportunity. She turned and kicked with all of her might. Her foot connected with the point of the assailant's chin. The assailant's head snapped back into the glow of the moon. It was Claudia. Matilean charged like a raging bull. As Claudia was falling to the floor, Matilean tackled her into several boxes.

Victoria heard the noise and fell down the stairs. Meanwhile, Seth was making his way back outdoors when he heard, then saw, Victoria tumbling down the stairs. Victoria was happy to see him.

"Brotha!" she screamed before she reached him.

He looked concerned, "What's wrong?"

"It's Matilean."

"What about Matilean? Where is she?"

She tried to catch patches of air as she confessed. "They're upstairs fighting."

"Who?"

"They jumped her, Claudia, Lilly, and Sabrina. I didn't wanna be a part of it, but they made me."

Seth didn't wait to hear another word before charging up the stairs.

The salt generated from Matilean's sweat had seeped into the fingernail cuts on her face, it burned, but she had more serious problems to worry about. During the scuffle, she had fallen between Claudia's large thighs. Claudia crossed her legs around Matilean's rib cage and squeezed like a boa constrictor. In retaliation, Matilean dug her nails into Claudia's face, but to no benefit. With legs like a man and with enough force, Claudia could fracture Matilean's ribs. The thought had run through her mind of doing exactly that. Matilean felt the pain and screamed. In desperation she sank her teeth into Claudia's neck. Claudia's body shifted, squirmed, and wiggled before the pressure around Matilean's waist abated.

Claudia's newest effort was trying to get Matilean off her neck. No matter how hard she tugged at Matilean's hair, Matilean's teeth and jaws were clinched tightly into her neck similar to a pit bull lioness locked on its prey. Her razor sharp teeth bit deeper and deeper into Claudia's neck. She heard Claudia's cry, felt her desperate punches on the back of her head, and Claudia's nails clawing her sides, but she clinched tighter and tighter to her neck.

Seth burst through the door and flipped the switch on the wall. Right in front of his sight was Lillian and Sabrina out cold, then his gaze turned to Claudia's wailing. He reached for Matilean's waist and pulled.

"Let go, Mat. Let go," he commanded.

Finally the vampire broke her seal and blood ran from her lips. She wanted to pounce back on Claudia and even attempted to, but Seth caught her and carried her out of the room, up the hall, and into the bathroom.

Claudia's face wore defeat; she had had no idea who she was up against. She breathed heavily as her body stretched out with relief. Victoria stood in the entrance of the doorway, and snickered; perhaps Claudia had learned her lesson. Had she been brave enough to fight Claudia, she would have. Victoria's heart went out to Matilean; she had betrayed her and she could sense Matilean's disappointment.

Betrayal is hurtful and leaves an ugly scar. This can last a lifetime if not treated. Victoria wanted so much to say I'm sorry, but halfway to the bathroom guilt made her turn away.

Seth sat on the commode with Matilean still cradled in his arms like a baby. He ran some water and softly wiped the blood from her face. Claudia had left some personal carvings on Matilean's face.

"Why y'all fightin'?"

"You know why we fightin'."

"How did you manage to get in the house?"

"Victoria. We was looking fo you. Well, I was looking fo you and that girl."

"Who, Sabrina?"

"Yeah, Sabrina."

"After what happened, I guess you know I wasn't with her. Anyway, you ok?"

"Now, I am."

"I was afraid this would happen," Seth admitted.

"So was I. I just hope that is the end of it."

"I got a good feelin' it is. Looks as if Claudia left some battle scars, it's nothing that time can't heal. You'll be ok."

Matilean saw the moment as an opportunity to petition once again for her cause. "In time just about anything is able to heal, but some things need to want healing." She paused and looked directly at him. "Seth what do you want? Tell me."

Seth closed his eyes as her hands grazed over his cheeks. "I wish all this would just go away—me arguing with my dad, my sista fighting with you." When his eyes opened so did his soul.

"Do you wish I was gon?" she asked.

"Not you, but the circumstance, yes."

In half a second, she got the notion to kiss him. "I love you, Seth," she said, after kissing him. "If I had one wish to my name, I would give it to you."

She snuggled into his chest. "Hold me, Seth." She wanted his comfort, and he rocked her until her stare was fixated on the wall behind him.

"Sometimes you do things without thinking 'bout the consequences," she said with a blank expression, "but the impact is painful, worse than any yo sista could deliver. The moment you think life is great, the repercussions blindside you just like she did. Many a night I cried myself to sleep wishin' all this had not happened. I listen to my mother preach about joy comin' in the mornin'. The only thing I get in the mornin' is reality. And it ain't joyful. I'm beginning to wonder if happiness got me in its plans."

"Sure it do, Mat. You talkin' as if our predicament is permanent."

"Isn't it?" she snapped.

"I'm continually being told that happiness is what you make it. PT said times get rough, things happen, people make mistakes, but life don't stop." He reiterated, "Life don't end 'cause you make a mistake."

"Already made too many mistakes, and don't got no room left to make no more."

He knew what she meant by the comment and decided to change the subject.

"Mat, befo you knew me what was your impression of me?"

Her frown eased. "Oh, I always thought you was stuck on yoself. I neva thought of it as a problem 'cause I always liked a confident guy. But since our problem, yo confidence and courage ain't nowhere to be found."

She knew what he was doing, and she refused to allow him to brush the issue off, as if it were some trivial mishap.

"Ok, you getting' way too deep. Why you persist on going back to this?" asked Seth.

"It's not going away 'cause we want it to go away. Plus, I wanna make sure I'm getting' my point across." She wanted to have the last word. "Ain't I got a say in all this?"

Seth gave Matilean a sharp look without answering.

"If I do, I can't tell. My feelings and opinions seem to go unheard." She pulled herself from his lap and stood. He talked as she looked in the mirror to study the swelling on her face.

"As much as you don't want me to believe it, I do have a say in this, too," answered Seth. He looked at her through the mirror and continued, "Why you think I'm gettin' you to go to West Virginia? This ain't all fo me. I'm tryin' to help you, too."

"Seth, I know ya think ya helping me by getting me to do this. But I don't know. I neva meant to overstep my boundaries by comin' ova heah. If I had somewhere else to go I would. Nothin' worse than being in a place ya not wanted and there's nothin' that I can do 'bout it. I am at yo family's mercy 'cause I know my mother is unmerciful. I have seen and felt it. Seth can'tcha hea what I am tellin' ya? I need ya bad right now. Ya all I got. Ya say ya not like yo father, but this matter ya won't discuss with him. When I look at ya right now, I don't want to see yo father. I don't wanna hea his awful words. But the truth is that you're worse than yo father. At least he stood up fo what he believes.

"I'm nothing like my father. You turn everything around. You make it sound like I'm a coward, like I'm spineless because I don't stand on this side of the fence or that side of the fence. Or because I don't scream I am black to the first white person I see. Or protest my father for his beliefs about dark people. I am a black man. I never thought I was blacker than the darkest man or lighter than the lightest black man. I know I'm black, Mat, and neither yo family or mine is gon tell me any different."

"Seth, I'm not questioning your blackness," she paused to consider this before she said it, "only your manhood."

"I'm a man, no matter what ya think. I got a question for ya. You tell yo momma 'bout me?"

"Yes, Seth, I did."

"If I recall, you lied to yo mother about me, jus' as I lied to my father 'bout you, so what makes you any different from me?"

"I lied because of love, Seth, and would hope you did the same, but yo constant excuses make it clear ya lied because of fear."

"A lie is a lie, Mat. But you quick to throw the first stone. You lied out of fear, just like I did."

Vaguely, she remembered telling her mother about Seth. Well, she told her mother about a guy, a guy who needed tutoring after school. With a straight face, she told her mother that he was a good Christian boy who attended United Baptist over on South Hawkins Street. Of course, it was the only way she could meet with Seth.

Matilean sat and thought about the lies she'd told. The lie actually worked, she thought, because the boy's credentials passed the test. Her mother would never allow her to associate with a non-Christian boy, especially one from the north side of town.

She didn't want to believe that her lies upheld the same beliefs as her mother, but, shamefully, she dropped her head, knowing Seth was right. The weight of it all: the lies, the constant fighting, the pressure of acceptance, and the search for security rested in her belly.

Her gaze went deeper into his face. She realized that she had just as much responsibility to share her pregnancy with her mother as Seth did with his father.

"I guess my mother is no different than yo father."

"What you mean to say is you no different than me. You always screamin' 'bout tradition and breaking tradition; yet, you met with the same practices, but I don't see you making no attempts to break'em. You and yo mother kill me with that holier-than-thou stuff. How she gon preach goodwill but act mean-spirited?"

A storm was brewing in her head. Her thoughts gathered as cumulous clouds. The more Seth ranted, the denser her thoughts became.

His words bit deep like teeth, and she felt them latch onto her heart. "Listen, I am tired of havin' this conversation." Then Seth stormed out the bathroom.

She closed the door behind him and took a seat on the commode. Seth had gotten his point across again, and she was left feeling like the villain. He often left her in that state of mind, wondering what she could do or say to satisfy his position rather than thinking of ways to support her own.

Lately, at every opportunity Seth and Matilean met, tragedy had been meeting with them. She thought she could learn to deal with it and all its surprises. Well no more, enough was enough. Why fight it any longer? She considered getting rid of the baby to eradicate all her problems. With the baby gone, things would be back like they were. That would certainly make Seth happy, but from Matilean's perspective such a thing neither would nor could offer her happiness. A bold decision that at one point she refused to contemplate was now actually being considered. She agreed with herself to tell him.

Slight movements coming from the ceiling caused Matilean's head to abruptly tilt upward. She knew someone or something was coming and she chose not to hang around to find out. She headed back to the hallway very aware, remembering to look around the dark corners in case Claudia was attempting a second assault.

As Matilean approached the flickering light in the hallway, a hidden door with no outside handle plopped open. She caught her breath as her weapons raised through the air. She hoped Claudia wasn't behind the door. Deep inside her core, she believed she had at least an ounce of fight left. The rest would be up to Claudia. The damage to her body may only have been flesh wounds. Maybe, the real fight was just getting started.

Peeking from behind the door was Biff, a welcomed sign of relief for Matilean. He grabbed her by her good wrist and pulled her into the tight dark space. He reached into the black space, confident to strike the light cord. The light illuminated a twisted staircase similar to that under the stage at her school.

Biff walked down the steps with confidence, clinging only to gravity. Matilean held on to his shoulders. The old stairs cracked and complained with the placement of each foot. As she walked the steps, she thought about her encounter with Seth under the staircase. Trusting someone else on a twisted staircase occupied her mind. Before she could weigh the thought, she saw an approaching light.

She could tell that Biff knew this house better than anyone, including Old Man Woodson. She accepted the fact that the movements in the bathroom were spawned by Biff. She knew that Biff overheard her conversation with Seth. How much he heard, she couldn't be certain. When she saw the light her suspicions of Biff were eased.

Biff led her into a sizeable country kitchen, with hanging pots and pans, a two-piece kitchen cupboard and cabinet, a dinette table, a large refrigerator, and a gas burner stove. She was amazed to see that the kitchen had a matching kitchen table set, a twin pail for cleaning floors, a four-piece canister set, and a long handled dust pan, which would definitely come in handy in her house. Trying to find a cardboard to get up that last bit of dirt was time consuming, she thought.

Matilean was quick to notice an additional wood stove closely placed near the center wall. It actually reminded her of their wood-burning stove.

A long, inverted L-shape tin neck connected from the wall to the back of the stove. Biff dashed over to the sink and crashed to his knees. He opened the bottom doors and extracted a pickle jar without the pickles. In place of the pickles was a concoction of nasty, murky looking water and decaying peaches and apples. When Biff twisted the top off, the foul smell of rotten preserves bit their nostrils.

Matilean grimaced while covering her nose, "That stinks."

Biff presented a mischievous smirk as he caught two renegade roaches racing by his knees.

"No, you not doing what I think you gon do?" solicited Matilean. "Don't."

"Don't worry, they won't notice the difference. The roaches will give it mo flavor."

And so he dropped the two roaches in with the peaches and apples.

"Aren't you supposed to be cookin' Momma some food? She was complaining, sayin' she ain't got it yet. You betta get to cookin' 'cause this is the last of the wine."

"I thought she had passed out."

"She woke up because she got thirsty and I got this to help quench her thirst," he said, while raising the jar, then searching for more things to put into the wine.

Matilean grabbed the largest cooking pot she could find and slid it across the kitchen table. Even though Matilean was apprehensive about cooking, she knew that beef stew wasn't a hard meal to prepare. She had watched her mother prepare it plenty of times. As she searched for the various ingredients needed for the stew, she soon learned that Edna's kitchen didn't have the same ingredients her mother would use. Therefore, she would have to make the necessary substitutes. She peeled and chopped and tossed it all in the large pot. The flavoring would give her the most difficult test. Her mother knew the exact measurements without the aid of a teaspoon or measuring cup. Too much of one thing and not enough of another could ruin the stew. That's what she didn't need. She opened the cabinet where the spices were kept.

To her surprise, Edna had about twenty different spices, but she recognized only two, salt and pepper. She decided to rely on a custom of the elders—trial and error—to help her season the stew. She offered up a prayer for extra taste.

The only thing left was to slow cook the stew. Matilean looked around for the stove. Biff turned around to watch her.

"What are you doing?"

"Looking fo the stove," she answered. He gave her a confused expression then pointing to one corner of the room, "The stove is ova' there."

She walked over to the stove, and confusingly, she peered down at the burners. She wasn't familiar with a gas stove. "How do you work it?"

"Turn it on," he gestured with his hand toward the knobs protruding from the front of the stove. He turned his attention back to the jar. Matilean apprehensively switched on one of the knobs. The burner gave off a quiet hiss. She watched for something to happen. The flame still did not appear. A couple of minutes went by and still there was no flame. The hissing broke Biff's concentration and he jumped and ran over to the stove. He flipped the handle back to its off position.

"You never worked a gas stove?"

"Nope."

"Well, you gon blow us up. After you cut it on, you gotta take a match to light the burner. Then the flame will pop on. You leave the gas on too long before lighting it then..." he smacked the table with his hand to heighten the dramatics. "Ka Boom! Even I'm not brave enough to blow us up."

"How long do the gas have to stay on befo it goes Ka Boom?" Matilean asked, without the special effects.

"I don't know, and I don't want to find out. I tell ya what, go ahead and use the kitchen wood stove. You do know how to use that?"

She rolled her eyes and used her lips to let off a loud smack. "Yeah, I know how to use a wood stove, but it'll take a long time to cook."

Matilean tossed in a few nearby logs. When the neck of the stove turned scarlet red, she panicked. The stew could cook too fast, she thought. Biff reached up to open the air vent on the wood stove.

When there was nothing else to add to the wine, Biff closed the top and rose to his feet. He stopped in the small hallway that led to the kitchen. He commented back to Matilean, "Don't worry, this will hold her ova for a few."

She was open to Victoria's idea of cooking as a means to getting her in the house. Now another opportunity, she thought. Suddenly, much like a spring rain, ideas began to drizzle through her mind. Eleanor, her aunt who lived next door, relished old myths. And she passed them on to Matilean. Aunt Eleanor preached, "The way to a man's heart is through his stomach." Aunt Eleanor even went further and said, "Drop a bit of blood in his spaghetti and you got'im fo life."

Matilean wished she had fixed some spaghetti instead of the stew, but it was too late now. She figured the stew would have to do and without the blood.

The ingredients solidified before bubbling like hot lava. She bent over the pot and took several sniffs, hoping not to detect anything singed.

CHAPTER 13

1:35 a.m.
Sunday Morning

Seth was on the phone with Dr. McCray from West Virginia. He tried talking quickly before anyone came along.

"Yes sir, I know it's late. Yes, I got the extra two hundred dollars. She'll be on time. Sure." Seth paused to check around himself, "Dr. McCray, I was thinking, this procedure that you do, it's not gon hurt Matilean, is it?"

He talked a few minutes more before softly returning the receiver to its base. His heartbeat returned to its normal beat. He couldn't pretend he didn't understand the gravity of what he wanted her to do. A small gain could mean a great loss. Now, he wasn't sure if he even wanted her to do it. As Seth pushed the thought to the back of his mind Biff walked past holding the jar of wine.

"Where you going with that?" asked Seth.

"It's for Momma."

Seth reached for the jar, "Naw, she don't need no more of this stuff."

Biff was quicker in preventing Seth from grabbing it. "I don't want her mad at me, so once I give it to her you can take it away from her. Then she can hit you up side yo head. I don't see no reason why I got to take yo lick." Biff smiled and continued through the foyer.

"Wait a minute," demanded Seth, "have you seen Matilean?"

"She not in my pockets."

Even though the remark was silly, Seth caught himself looking at Biff's pockets.

"Biff, you don't have no pockets."

"That's why she ain't in'em. She might be walkin' down the street. She was upset after ya'll's argument in the bathroom. "

"You were hiding in the attic, listening won't you?"

Seth followed him to the porch. He figured taking the alley would cut Matilean off before she reached the tracks.

"How long ago, Biff?"

"About ten minutes ago." Biff enjoyed sending people on wild goose chases.

"This better not be one of yo tricks, Biff."

Eddie yelled uncontrollably, as Seth walked onto the porch. "She's heah, Seth."

"Who's here? Eddie, you pissy drunk."

"That girl, ya know from yo last party!"

"Eddie, calm down and stop yelling."

"Ok, I saw her from a distance, but I'm sure it's her. Even looks like her except for her hair. It looks like it's been cut. Eddie grinned, "She looking good, Seth."

"That's good, Eddie, but I can't talk right now."

"Where you going?" Eddie called. "I haven't told you the rest."

"Tell me later."

Seth slipped down the steps and ran towards the alley.

Biff tapped Edna on the shoulder before he noticed Old Man Woodson's Nova creeping slowly along the front of the house with its headlights off. Edna's hand swiped for Biff to put the jar down. Before Biff could place the jar on the floor he screamed, "Uh oh, Daddy!" It was warning enough for him to take off running and leave the jar suspended in the air; then it crashed to the floor: peaches, apples, and the two roaches, still alive, scattered with all the able-bodied partygoers. Those bodies that couldn't flee would have to take their chances surviving the monsoon that was coming inland. Even PT and Ophelia were wise to get out of the path of destruction by taking cover in the lilacs and tulips underneath the banister.

Biff ran through the foyer, through the living room and into the kitchen. He entered with such urgency, that Matilean assumed Edna was upset that the stew wasn't finished.

"I bet yo mother is ready for the stew."

Even Biff wasn't evil enough to send Matilean out into the storm that was building with each step, moving straight towards the house. Biff paused to think. In that time, he argued with his conscious about warning Matilean of Old Man Woodson's presence. His conscience did not win.

He naughtily smiled, "Yep, she wants it now!" Then he peeled out the back door.

The stew was practically done when the illusion of hope circled around in her head. Maybe she wasn't as fed up as she thought, maybe she could hold on until Seth ate the stew, then maybe he'd see what he was missing. She played with the thought while stirring the ingredients in the pot. "It smells good," she admitted softly. "Coming up is some of the best beef stew Mrs. Woodson and Seth will eva taste."

Matilean desired to look as sweet as the food smelled. A glare in the kitchen window reflected her image; she took a moment to make sure her hair and clothes were in place before taking the stew out to Edna.

Old Man Woodson flung and shoved legs, arms, backs, butts, heads, and chests of both men and women to reach his porch. He added an occasional kick, spit, and yank to make his travels easier. Behind him lay massive devastation and wounded bodies.

One could plainly hear the grinding of his teeth. He saw his stereo holding up records, ashtrays, and empty beer cans. Eddie had taken off, leaving a record still spinning.

Edna looked up long enough to drool like a baby before passing out again. Disgusted, he couldn't be silent. He uttered harsh profanity.

Unaware of Old Man Woodson's presence on the porch, Matilean backed out the screen door with the pot of stew close to her chest. She wasn't aware that he was standing in her path. When she turned, the two collided face to face. The pot simply slipped out of her hands into his. Old Man Woodson's hot liquor breath burned her face. He didn't have to say a word; his eyes said it for him. His thirst for food made him grab the handle of the spoon. With one heaping gulp, he swallowed the stew. A few seconds later, he regurgitated stew, liquor, and chunks of a roast beef sandwich he'd eaten three hours earlier. He walked with the pot over to the banister and dumped out its contents. Before it could hit the flowers and the earth, it poured over Ophelia's head and slipped down her back. The stew burned. PT slapped his hand across her mouth to keep her from screaming.

Old Man Woodson looked hatefully at Matilean, "Who in the hell told you you could cook?"

Matilean cautiously pointed to Edna without taking her eyes from Old Man Woodson's. He grimaced at the sight of his wife stretched out in the chair. It inflamed his rage.

"I didn't ask you that," he roared, then shoved the pot hard into Matilean's chest.

Immediately her wind escaped her lungs, clasping her chest. In front of Old Man Woodson, Matilean's courage had become thinner, more porous, and susceptible to fracture. She quivered in her stance, she knew without a doubt that Old Man Woodson was going to kill her at that very moment. She wondered where Seth was.

He repeated his question, "Who told you you could cook?"

Matilean quickly lifted her head to answer him. Her words were running and stumbling, "No-body."

"Den why the hell you in my kitchen cookin' that nasty shit?" he growled.

She didn't know how to answer him. Old Man Woodson screamed in her face, "Did you hea what I said, gal?"

Her not answering him quickly was an insult to him and fed his rage.

"What part of yo black ass didn't understand when I told you to neva go past that gate? Huh?"

She didn't answer. She just waited for the inevitable.

"Answer me, gal!"

Without warning, his large hand swiftly came through the air like she expected.

He looked down at Matilean, who barely ducked the sweeping blow. She had one hand up protecting her face and the other clutching the handle on the pot. His hand smacked the wall hard. Frustrated, he disgustedly nudged her out of the way with his foot as he entered the house. He made sure the screen door slammed behind him. She exhaled a feeling of relief after having a brush with death.

After Old Man Woodson cursed her, she wanted to leave, but she realized she didn't have anywhere to go. She picked up her pride and took it around to the side of the house. Tate was stretched out on the sofa so she sat in a small chair and watched dawn turn into day.

When Seth didn't see Matilean at the path, he figured she was heading over to Iva's house. He was hesitant about going across the tracks at such a late hour. But for whatever reason he wanted her back and he knew he had to go across the tracks to retrieve her.

CHAPTER 14

14 minutes to 6:00 a.m.
Sunday Morning

Random thoughts left her vaguely saddened while sitting on the side of the house watching the sun peek its face over the horizon. Charmed and hypnotized by the coloration of the sun's beauty, Matilean sank deeper into the chair. "How much more beautiful a sunrise could be if I wasn't weighed down with so many problems," she spoke aloud.

"It's beautiful, isn't it?"

Matilean snapped from her trance and immediately sat upright. She hadn't seen Mrs. Woodson since she fell asleep in the chair. The sunshine crept across Mrs. Woodson's lips and up along her cheekbones. As she turned her head to block out the sun's rays, she waved for Matilean to come sit with her on the sofa.

"Yes'um," replied Matilean, then noticing Tate had vanished from the sofa.

A cool morning breeze twisted in from the field, ruffled the hedges, and settled down on a caterpillar moving slowly across the wooden planks that laced the porch. In sudden defense, the caterpillar balled into a knot. Mrs. Woodson noticed the caterpillar and studied its size and the lines on its back.

"Fall coming soon." Matilean followed Mrs. Woodson's eyes to the curled up caterpillar. Mrs. Woodson continued, "A caterpillar is to fall what the ground hog is to spring, but you don't hear no one making a big fuss ova a maggot, no one hunting fo it to take its picture." She directed with a pointing finger, "Look at dem dark orange lines on its back. Dem lines let you know how soon fall will be heah." She strained to make out the number of lines on the caterpillar's back. "Baby, my eyes ain't what they used to be, do an old lady a favor and count dem lines."

The breeze had let up. The caterpillar stretched into full stride, inching its way to the edge of the porch.

"Three and what looks like a half of a line."

Mrs. Woodson's eyes rolled to the right corner of her head, to process the data in accordance with the old rituals. Once completed, "Well, fall will be here in three to four weeks, and winter will be a cold one," she added.

Matilean returned her stare back to the field and the light wind that lifted dirt and debris into the air just to resettle it. She would have rather studied Mrs. Woodson's face and whatever hidden secrets she may have locked up in her head. Like Mrs. Woodson studied the caterpillar, she would have studied Mrs. Woodson's few lines of age that ran along the outside of her face and disappeared underneath her chin.

What she would have given to know her methods for staying so young and beautiful. If she could have truly looked at Mrs. Woodson, she might have com-

pared the paradigm of that caterpillar and the process
of its metaphoric change into a butterfly with the fil-
tering of generations that diluted the African culture
into a dark-white subculture. She would have studied
Mrs. Woodson's eyes to understand why the window
of her soul was closed to the idea of accepting the
unaccepted. She would have studied the person and
allowed the sun's rays to reveal her hidden wonders.

Mrs. Woodson continued to stare at the caterpillar, then said, "You know, what the caterpillar looks at
as the end of the world, the butterfly looks at as a new
beginning. So, what do you see?"

Unconsciously, Matilean was gazing into the side
of Mrs. Woodson's face.

"Sorry ma'am, I don't mean to stare."

"No need to apologize. I don't mind being studied
as long as ya learn something."

"I'm surprised," replied Matilean.

"Surprised?"

"Why, yes. Not meaning to sound blunt, but my
uncle drinks heavily and his skin is awful, but yours
is so beautiful and flawless."

Edna had already known the question that was
itching Matilean's tongue.

"The things we shouldn't do, we do, and the
things we should do, we don't. Ain't that what de
Bible say?"

"I guess." Matilean knew the passage because her
mother constantly repeated it. What she didn't know
was Edna's purpose for citing it. She sat quietly and
listened.

"What the Bible don't tell ya is that reality is painful, very painful. Even when ya do all that ya can do,
it ain't enough. Even when ya put yo soul into loving,

it still ain't enough." She gazed into the field as the mental pain resurfaced to her face. "And the pain inside is so unbearable that it can only be suppressed with an artificial love."

"Mrs. Woodson, it's not my place to say, but why you talk such things? I saw yo strength."

Edna had a lonesomeness that was concealed with alcohol, but never filled with love. Examining an empty wine bottle half buried in the hedge bush, she pointed with her stare, "That bottle is the only strength I've eva known."

She looked at Matilean with bitterness trapped in her heart. Her face looked desperate to tell someone her pain. "Everybody wants to be somebody that they're not." Mrs. Woodson gazed back into the field, "Life is much like that pile of dirt. Ya get settled and comfortable to what life offers. Sometimes life is fair and sometimes it ain't. 'Casionally, there are situations or a person that comes along to stir up things. Much like that cool breeze moving that dirt from one place to another. It's nothin' the dirt can do but go along with the ride. When it settles, sometimes the dirt and dust collects itself, sometimes it don't, but one thing is for sho, it will be in a different place. Well, regardless of the place, it's said that God neva gives you somethin' you can't handle."

Matilean began to panic, she wasn't sure if Edna was referring to herself as the person who would stir up things. She considered Seth telling Edna about the baby; maybe Biff, he was snooping in the bathroom. If he did, that would be a burden off of her, or what if that entire story was just another way to persuade her to get rid of the baby, she thought nervously.

Matilean had a thousand questions for Edna, but she didn't know if it would upset her, so her fear of upsetting Edna restrained her tongue from asking.

The sound of music, like the smell of freshly baked bread, floated through the open air and tantalized the two of them. Adjacent to the house was a church that sat in the open field. On a perfect day, the organ could be heard for miles around. That morning, a cool breeze carried the piano's high and low ripples to ears that sat on neighboring porches. It had been a long time since Matilean heard the sweet sound of gospel music.

"How sweet that sound is," Edna remarked and then continued, "it's sweet like Tapioca puddin', ain't it?"

"Yes'um, I guess. I neva had Tapioca puddin'."

Edna playfully slapped Matilean's knee, "Sometimes, I like to come out heah and listen to what God is talkin' 'bout."

Hesitantly, she asked, "You can hear'im?"

Mrs. Woodson chuckled. She placed her hand over her heart, "You hear him in heah. He speaks to yo heart by way of yo conscience, suga."

"Conscience?" replied a confused Matilean.

"Ya do know right from wrong?"

"Yes'um, I know."

"God uses yo conscience to keep you from doing wrong. He at least allows you to think about what you gonna do befo you do it. Wished he had spoke quicka befo I did some of my sins."

"But you said he did."

"He did, but the devil spoke a little louda, suga." She gave Matilean another pat on the thigh. "And the Lord knows, I did enjoy some of dem sins."

"Why do you prefer to listen out heah rather than going into the church?"

"Suga, God is not limited. He's out heah just as he is in that church. I'm just one hypocrite excluded from the congregation," she loudly announced.

"My momma says even though God is everywhere you need a main servant to help teach you how to find him."

"Well, when God is ready for me, he'll find me right on this heah poach. I hope he don't come back like the Good Book say."

"How is that?"

"'As a thief in the night,' 'cause the Lord knows that's when I'm at my worst."

Matilean tried to hold in her laughter but found her efforts useless. Interestingly enough, she took a liking to Mrs. Woodson. Matilean realized that everybody has their ways, but Edna was genuinely honest about what she said and did. That was a rare trait in most people, thought Matilean.

"Listen baby, temples are good to have, they are places to worship, but the most important temple is the one you carry 'round every day, and don't you foget it. When God is ready for ya, he's likely to use anyone to reach ya. And don't worry, he'll find ya."

Then Edna switched subjects, "Baby, yo momma know where ya are?"

"Yes'um," she lied. Edna smiled because she knew Matilean was lying.

"Ya been ova heah all night, I'm sho she's worried."

"No ma'am, she's not worried."

"Well, where you live?"

"Capital Heights."

"That's 'round the corner from Sunshine Market?"

Matilean was surprised that she knew. "Yes'um, right by First Street."

"I know, right down the street."

"How did you know that?" asked Matilean.

"Well, hell's fire. We used to live by de park. You know whar I'm talkin' 'bout?"

"Yes'um. It's still there."

"I know it's still thar, I was just ova thar two days ago gettin' me some tatas and greens."

Then it came, that tickling on Matilean's tongue that drove her to ask. "You lived there?"

"Baby, all black folk lived thar sometime or 'nother." Edna laughed, "What, you think we was born and raised on this side of town?"

"But I thought you lived...."

Edna interrupted, "I used to live in the country, deep in the country, and if you wanted a job you had to go to the city. And God knows I was tired of livin' in the country, sloppin' hogs and tendin' to cows."

She stopped and adjusted herself for she was about to tell a story.

"When we first got heah, we moved to the city just like every other black folks seekin' work. Then the politicians started focing blacks outta the inner city away from the businesses. They had to put blacks somewhere. The majority of us blacks they moved to the south side of the city where you find the worst houses and livin' conditions."

Edna looked out into the field, "City din't care 'bout us, they din't want us livin' on the good land. Dat is, the land that they wanted for the new highway.

It all 'bout money, it always 'bout money, racism jus' a way to get the money through quicka. Lawd knows we had it bad jus' like every other black tryin' to get somethin' with nothin'. Hopin' that somethin' would be a little betta than what we already had."

She paused for a minute to listen to the tinkling keys of the piano. Matilean felt the sharpness of the morning breeze and the sharpness of Edna's words against her face.

"Black folks started movin' ova heah 'round the forties. This used to be a rich naborhood in the twenties and thirties, then it turned into an all white, workin' class naborhood. When we moved ova heah, a few rich people were still heah, but after the war, they, too, moved out past the city. And the new highway took'em and the jobs."

She snapped her arm forward to point out a few houses in the neighborhood that had previously been vacated by white residents.

A few neighbors sat on their porches, but Matilean had a hard time figuring if the new occupants were black since they looked so white.

"Jus' the thought of blacks movin' in these nahborhoods is causin' mo of'em to move out, soon won't nothin' but blacks be livin' ova heah. Damn realtors done destroyed a lot of these homes."

Matilean quietly listened to Edna rave on about the government and plans for more development that meant more blacks would be displaced.

Matilean saw another side of Edna, one of compassion. She no longer considered that Edna harbored the same beliefs as Old Man Woodson. She had no idea of the path that struggles take people, but Edna had taken hers and it kind of gave Matilean hope. She had assumed from their house, their pretty cars, and their complexion that they had experienced less hardship and pain.

Betsy Morgan heard their voices and appeared breast first. "I thought I heard some voices ova heah. Edna, whatcha got fo a splittin' headache?"

"Another drink," laughed Edna.

"I pass. My head feels like somebody took a sledgehammer to it." She abruptly grabbed her side, "Somethin' bit the eva livin' hell out of my side."

She revealed the wound that had swollen and turned purple overnight.

Edna examined the wound up close. "I don't know what could've bit you to make that mark."

A steel needle, thought Matilean.

"And to top it off, I don lost my damn wig again. At da last party, Biff glued it on ya dog's head."

Edna giggled, "It took two hours to get dat thing off Rimy."

Matilean laughed and asked, "He glued it on who? Rimy?"

"How he got dat dog to stay still long enough fo'im to do it is beyond me. Betsy should've thrown that old thing away long time ago. It's 'bout time you bought a new one."

"New? That's the same wig I lost befo. 'Der was so much glue in it I was forced to cut mos' of the wig."

"Betsy, that can't be the same wig as befo, no way."

"Sure is, girl, I looked good wit shart hair."

Matilean didn't know if it was a question or a statement so she looked at Betsy's appearance compared to what she remembered. The old short, patchy gray hair was definitely no match for the uneven bushy wig from last night.

"Girl, I'm goin' home. If my wig turns up, call me and I'll send one of dem lazy kids of mine to fetch it." She stopped, then asked, "Where is Seth so he can take me home?"

"Dem poke woodcutters left Tate passed out on the sofa; after Tate woke up I made Seth drive'im home. But, that was some time ago. Hang around fo a few, he'll be back."

"Nawl, I ain't got da time to waste. I got ta clean, cook, and curse my kids out for not cleanin' and cookin'. 'Minds me, I gotta go ta the market for some poke chops, some split pea soup wit some smoke poke and a bag of taters. 'Dey gotta 10 lb bag for 39 cent. Ya wan' me ta pick ya up a bag?"

"Nawl, I'm good fo now."

"How 'bout some starch. 'Dey got that fo twenty-four cent ah pack."

"Yeah, pick me up a box, Biff ate the last of it. By the way, the number was seven fifty."

"Seven fifty," she turned to walk away. "Damn."

"What?" asked Edna.

"Seven fifty in the dream book is wig."

They listened to Betsy Morgan drag herself away with complaints and moans until she could no longer be heard.

"Mrs. Woodson," whispered Matilean.

"Yes, baby."

"I was sittin' next to Tate, but I didn't hea Seth move'im."

"Child, you was dead to the world sleep. I told Seth he bet not wake you. Don't worry, he be back to walk ya home."

"Mom," Biff's voiced sirened!

"What do that boy want now, jus' a lot of unnecessary yellin'. If you gon yell, yell fo somethin'—like the house burning down. Don nothin' drive my nerves as much as someone screamin' and don want nothin'. Go ahead and scream, I'm not movin' from this heah seat."

Matilean laughed and to her surprise Mrs. Woodson joined her. Biff's voice sirened to the point it irritated both Matilean and Mrs. Woodson, to the point Mrs. Woodson was compelled to check on him.

"Damn it to hell, let me go in heah and see what dis boy wants." Quickly, Matilean rose too.

"No suga, you stay right thar and enjoy some of the peacefulness the Lord has given us on such a beautiful Sunday mornin', Lawd knows I can't."

Matilean sank back into her seat. Peace was far from her reach. Outside was silent, but her insides were erupting into a tantrum of nerves, and they were hard to reach like an itch in the middle of her back. She carefully caressed the tangible pain in her hand, which hurt to the touch. After being hit and hitting, she could barely wiggle her fingers.

She was surprised that Mrs. Woodson stayed and talked as long as she did. She almost wished she knew about the pregnancy. Perhaps she would find the courage to tell her. She gathered reasons for Mrs. Woodson's acceptance of the situation. She would understand, of course she would. She's a woman and mother too. She said it herself, 'People make mistakes, but we all need a second chance.' Matilean smirked with acceptance of her own rationality.

Her excitement suddenly disappeared when she realized upon whom her fate rested. No matter how much Matilean tried to convince herself, she knew the sole decision maker was not Mrs. Woodson. Matilean's mother was just as powerless. She figured the decision to kick Ruby out wasn't her mother's idea, but her stepfather's constant pressure from worrying about what it looked like to the neighbors and the church members to have an unwed, pregnant girl living in a Christian household.

He had a responsibility, and an image to uphold. He believed his duty was to protect Christianity, his family, and himself from what he considered the devil's temptations. His only remedy to the matter was ostracizing the person with the problem. Matilean was quite aware that Ruby's banishment was aimed at setting a precedent. Arguing against such a decision was futile in her family.

Matilean heard a man's voice in the distance. On the corner, an old, disheveled, and seemingly distraught man marched in a circle. In his hand he had a black Bible that he waved in the air. The old man's voice traveled low, then shot to a startling high. He screamed words of Jesus and faith. The voice pulled on Matilean, sitting her upright. She watched and waited. Never before had she witnessed a sidewalk preacher; the bystanders considered the man to be crazy. The music from the church had long stopped, so this stranger had her attention.

The voice growled then began to lift from a bellowing depth to a walloping pinnacle. Matilean focused on his words.

"What ever I've done, he's always there for me, yes, he is, I know."

Repeatedly, the voice moaned on. Even from a distance, Matilean could see the man's hand trembling uncontrollably as he turned the pages of the Bible.

He instructed those who watched to turn to The Acts of the Apostles Chapter 9 verses 1 through 9.

Matilean looked across the field to the neighboring porches. She expected to see people listening to the man, but much to her amazement, many of the adults paid no attention. A few children found him amusing.

He began to read from the Bible, " *'Meanwhile, Saul was still breathing out murderous threats against the Lord's disciples. He went into the high priest, and asked him for letters to the synagogues in Damascus, so that if he found any there who belonged to the Way, whether men or women, he might take them as prisoners to Jerusalem.'* "

Matilean listened intently to the man's voice resound off the houses. She waited for the stranger to break out with a loud scream about the passage. Or how God was planning to convict and cast all not following his law into the lake of eternal fire. So her stepfather had told her on many occasions. Instead, the preacher spoke softly.

"Most of us are like Saul," said the preacher, "what will it take for you to change?"

Somehow his topic had struck her personally. Inside of herself, she knew there were a lot of things that needed to change, but why now, she was young and had the rest of her life to change. Still the message wouldn't go away.

"A person will not change unless the pain of remaining the same hurts worse than the pain to change. Some of you don't want to change because you ain't hurting bad enough," said the preacher.

"That's why you're in a storm, but I'm here to tell you, God will send a storm to save you. You may be thinking God has abandoned you, but all he needs to say is Peace, be still."

"Please be quiet," a child's voice came from a nearby porch.

"But you must also understand that the peace comes from Christ within to handle the situation, even if the circumstance does not change. You have to trust God."

"Faith," a high tenor voice screamed.

"God intends for the storm to help you grow, so you can't stop working once the storm has gone," testified the stranger.

The message was touching her deeply and she felt a desire to close her eyes and pray, but neighboring stares and whispers prevented her from doing so. Instead, she allowed her eyes to look towards the sky without tilting her head too high.

CHAPTER 15

15 minutes after 9:00 a.m.
Sunday Morning

The late summer breeze started to chip away the loose paint around the edge of the windowsill at the back of the side porch. Victoria was sweeping her bedroom when an antagonizing tapping drove her crazy. A loose shutter dangled outside her window. She placed the broom in one of the corners of the room and headed towards the window. The morning sunlight beamed through the window across the room, exposing the lint that drifted freely. A few more bangs into the window increased her need to fix the shutter immediately. With no more effort than to lift the window and close the shutters, she stopped. Cautiously, she stretched the shutter outward and watched.

Victoria turned towards the sky to see what phenomenon was about to occur. She held her eyes there for a second then returned them back to Matilean.

Matilean was so engrossed in thought that she had long been unable to hear the stranger's voice. She wanted to cry out, but she knew the neighbors were watching to laugh at her expense. She dropped her eyes and her head to conceal her face. The words of the stranger lay upon her heart. A soft touch on her shoulder sent chills down her spine.

"God," she said, while hunched over, too ashamed to even look up, "I thought you only came as a thief in the night."

"I'm not God, Matilean," interrupted Victoria. "God would take up less space."

Victoria placed her small hand on Matilean's shoulder. The preacher had quieted down and a slight wind had renewed its circular rotation of lifting and replacing debris. Even the snooping neighbors soon gave up on seeing more entertainment. God may have designed another sign, but Matilean felt that God had his purpose for Victoria.

Sign or not, sudden bitterness leaped out of Matilean. She stood to her feet and, with her right hand, brushed Victoria's hand off her shoulder.

"What do you want?"

"I saw you from the window," she answered, then looked up at the window. "Are you ok?"

"What difference do it make to you?"

"I am sorry for last night. I wanted to tell you."

Matilean quickly interrupted her, "Well, why didn't ya? I guess our friendship wasn't strong enough for ya to protect me." She paused and looked into the field. "The only strength in this family rests on the one who hates the most." She didn't intend for Victoria to hear her insults of Old Man Woodson, but that's the way she felt and it just came out. Matilean quickly broke her daze to look at Victoria, "Don't fool yoself. You ain't my friend and ya neva was. You only an acquaintance and that's how I considered you. Friendship is built over time, so all that nonsense 'bout us being boon-coon buddies was a creation of yo imagination."

She wanted the words to hurt Victoria just like she was hurt last night, and they did. Victoria dropped her eyes and turned away. Matilean stopped her before she could see the back of her shoulders.

"I'm sorry Victoria, I didn't mean it."

Victoria was hesitant at first, but then she allowed the apology to take its effect.

"Matilean, I wanted to tell you but I was scared of what they would do to me. Can you forgive me?"

"I already did." She smiled and gave her a hug. Matilean needed the hug just as badly as Victoria did.

When it comes to the Woodsons, those of little faith would rightly be concerned for Matilean and Victoria, since both are denied any attention, respect, and consideration.

The two girls were gripped by a fear of overstepping their boundaries. Yet, they took the opportunity to realize and acknowledge the thing that controlled them also encouraged their ability to break free. In a sense, their friendship yielded a power that neither of them alone possessed.

The two sat quietly with their hands laced, ignoring the forbidden rules they had been taught all of their lives. They lingered in the comfort and courage of their closeness. If only for that moment, they sat there, pretending not to be afraid. In the house, Old Man Woodson wouldn't hesitate to inflict punishment on the two of them.

Victoria wrapped her arm around Matilean's shoulder, and gradually her eyes lifted to the top of Matilean's head. Victoria looked blankly out into the field until she heard the neighbors gathering

on their porches, giggling at the sight of the two of
them squeezed like sardines against one another. She
dropped her eyes in pity for them. Matilean, too, spotted the uninvited, nosy neighbors with their pointing
fingers and muttering words of rejection.

Thoughts of lying in her mother's arms, being
held tight, flashed in Matilean's mind. Again Matilean
assumed safety was in the arms of what would be
considered by her mother as the enemy.

For a moment she had forgotten what it felt like to
get that excited about something. The delight of the
feeling instantly pulled her from Victoria's clutch to
tell her about the preacher.

Victoria lifted her leg on the sofa then twisted her
body to face Matilean.

Matilean went on explaining to Victoria what the
preacher said and what she experienced.

"It was like a tingling sensation shot through my
entire body, I have neva felt such a feeling befo in my
life." She paused, "I can't explain it."

"I've been there," admitted Victoria.

"You have? But I thought…."

"I know. You think we don't believe in God."

Matilean dropped her eyes and said, "In a way,
yeah. Y'all neva talk about God and what he do. My
momma is always prayin' about this or that, anything
she needs, she looks to the Lord for it. Sometimes I
wonder why she prays so hard because we still in the
same place as most black folks; lower than the white
man and always depending on the white man for
something. I guess that's why I don't go to church all
that much. What our complexion gon get us?"

"I heard my momma pray a couple times,"
acknowledging some similarity. "It's usually ova

a porcelain toilet." They laughed. "But for her to believe God exists to help sober her gives me hope that he exists to keep her sober."

Matilean considered the feasibility of Victoria's statement compared to her own upbringing. Sporadically, Matilean would watch and listen to her mother give long prayers for security for both friends and foes, prosperity in the form of an extra twenty-five cents raise or enough money to purchase food, shelter, fuel, or clothes.

Victoria continued, "Momma don't know I listen. I pray that she would stop drinking, to stop allowing that bottle to abuse her and us. She gets drunk some-times and she just calls us all kinds of things. We ain't what she say we are," she said, to lessen the sting of the words Matilean had heard just hours before. "She knocks us down with cold words. I don't want her to be like that."

Too often Matilean was attacked with religious doctrine about how a young lady should conduct, control, and behave. This was her reason to rebel against all her mother's teachings.

Victoria continued, "Sometimes I know it's just the alcohol that makes her say a lot of those bad words and do such bad things. But when she's there on her knees puking all ova herself, praying for help, she gets my attention, and I don't care if it's the booze or not that makes her pray. I pray with her 'cause I want God to help her so bad. So it's not that we don't believe in God."

Matilean tried to rectify her statement. "No, I just thought y'all didn't rely on him as much as we do."

"Why? Because you think we rely more on our complexion to get us what we want? Some of us would argue that God gave us this complexion for a reason. Possibly this is our way of escaping so much unfairness."

Matilean tampered with the thought, "If y'all believe that, then why do y'all treat yo own kind the way you do?"

"Sometimes I feel like I got to, even if I don't want to."

Matilean could identify with her own willingness to succumb to deliberate attacks by quarrelsome girls.

"You should stand up fo what you believe in."

"Funny that you say that 'cause you didn't last night." Victoria had somehow culled out a weakness in Matilean's defense.

"Whatcha mean?"

"I mean when they talked about the darker blacks doing nothin' but havin' babies, you said nothing."

"They won't referring to me," she rebuked sharply.

"Yes they were and you knew it. I saw how you reacted."

"Well, what was I supposed to do?"

Boldly she said, "Stand up to'em."

Matilean renounced her defense, "Do you think all we do is have babies?"

"Look around Matilean. There are six of us so we can't talk about nobody sittin' 'round havin' babies. My uncle said befo my mother could drop a load, my daddy had already reloaded her."

What Victoria said was enlightening. It captured Matilean's attention. It would take something like feeling empty, lonely, and having a baby with nowhere to go, and no one to accept her, to make Matilean see the reality of life.

She lived in a world where cycles were inevitable: day turned into night, caterpillars into butterflies, seasons into seasons, and poverty, racism, and old traditions handed down from one generation to the next. Matilean wondered what it would take for someone like Mrs. Woodson to change. She was older, established with kids, shelter, and security. What grave consequences would she have to face in order to adopt a change of behavior?

Now that Matilean was sure she wanted to keep the baby, she didn't know what Seth's reaction would be. It was already planned and at any moment PT would be arriving to whisk her away to West Virginia. Seth expected her to go to a doctor she did not know, to have a procedure that could kill her both mentally and emotionally, and possibly physically. She knew that Seth would try hard to change her mind. And she wanted to be strong when he tried.

While she sat silently, staring into Victoria's fat cheeks and pale, light skin, she heard a voice in her head.

What are you thinking? What gleam of hope did you possibly give yourself to think you changing anything would make a difference? You have no idea what cost it's going to take. All the forbidden rules, traditional boundaries that were directly and indirectly, specifically and non-specifically stated, aren't going to disappear because you had a moment with God. Look at her skin.

Smooth like cream and as bright as the noon sun, it spells separation. How many times have her kind used your people, wasn't it she, your supposedly new friend that laughed at you, called you spook, jigaboo? And wasn't it she who betrayed you, and delivered you to the hands of your enemies? You will never be accepted and you will always be regarded as trash. Who do you trust? Indeed, it seems as if the music, singing, dancing, and preaching you heard was supposed to solve your problems. Are they solved? Are they gone? There are personal choices you must make which demand denying truths and concealing what you must do for the good of protecting yourself and your seed against them. Protecting your seed means removing your seed. Are you aware that even if you make every effort to conform to such a transformation means going through more hardship. You are not ready to handle that commitment. To a far greater degree, it rests on you to look perfect in the eyes of your mother. Having this baby will stain your appearance in her eyes. You will be forgotten. I've come to tell you what the truth is, so keep to your appointment.

To the minds of most, the mere presence of such a voice would have driven them straight off the edge. It wasn't yet determined if the voice clouded her sense of thoughts because, when she came to, Seth was standing over her, calling her name.

"What's wrong with you?" Then he looked at Victoria. "Victoria, what's wrong with her?"

"One moment we was talking and," slapping her own thigh, "I don't know. It's like she's under some spell."

Matilean swept her eyes up and along Seth's body.

"I'm ok. I jus' heard…I mean had a strange feeling."

Seth shrugged, "You sure you ok? I can get you some water."

"I'm ok. Don't you think I need to be getting off this porch befo yo daddy comes out?"

"Daddy's asleep, so don't worry 'bout that."

With a jerk of his hand and a nod from Seth, Victoria relinquished her seat. Matilean didn't notice the grin and a hand wave of departure by Victoria because she was busy contemplating what she heard or didn't hear. After a moment, Seth began to talk.

"Listen, I talked to PT and he's on his way ova to getcha," he said, in a hurry to explain the strategy before anyone could disrupt their meeting.

His voice stalled, "Umm," then remembering, "you gon complain about not havin' a ride home and he gon offer to take you 'cause he got to deliver some flowers to a customer in yo neighborhood. That way won't nobody question it," he added, as if convincing himself. "Now listen," he ordered as if she wasn't, "I already got the money to get this done. If the doctor ask how old you are you tell'im eighteen, you hea, eighteen?"

Matilean embraced the plan with a slow nod. Seth had turned four times and he was on his way to a fifth in search of PT's long Cutlass convertible.

Startled, "What?"

She tried to put aside what she just heard in her head and venture timidly into the forbidden conversation of keeping the baby. If she were unable to discuss it now then she would probably be coerced into going to West Virginia. She prayed to herself. Maybe her mother was somewhere praying and the strength from both their prayers would get her through this moment.

She chose to approach Seth with a story about a puppy her stepfather brought home when she was eight years old. Matilean told him there wasn't anything special about the puppy, he wasn't a thoroughbred—he was a mutt. Black and brown stripes scattered in all directions over his fur. It was apparent that the puppy was quite ill. He could barely walk without stumbling over his paws. And he couldn't hold anything in his stomach. The puppy's rib cage was visible through a thin coat of skin. Nasty mucous ran from both his eyes. Her stepfather made excuses for his sick looking appearance.

" 'He was the smallest in the litter, his brothas and sistas wouldn't allow it to eat, and he obviously contracted some kind of cold,' " my stepfather would add.

"He told me it was ugly, sick, and probably wouldn't live long. I asked'im why he brought it home.

"Speculating I didn't want it, my stepfather offered one reason. 'It is a gift to you.' I knew it was the prettiest puppy I had ever seen. Then I gave him reasons why I should keep the strange looking puppy, and how I would nurture it back to health. I threw my arms around the puppy's neck and smothered it with a big hug."

Matilean saw the bewildered expressions Seth made; he hadn't fully comprehended the meaning of the story. Risking even more of a chance for an argument, she went on explaining.

"Seth, my stepfather and I don't get along all that well, but he's the only father I know. Since I got ova heah yesterday, I realize his strict rules were only to protect me, jus' as yo father wants to protect you. I recall my stepfather saying, *some things people give you is worth keepin.'* He saw the respect in accepting a gift."

Seth shifted his head to take a peek at an empty street, "Go ahead, I'm listening."

"What I'm carrying inside me is a gift, a gift from God." She placed her hand over her stomach for emphasis.

"God?" Seth was unsure of the correlation.

"Yes, Seth, and I don't want to give our baby back or give our baby up. I know I can nurture this baby, provide for it, and help our baby grow. I know raising this baby is going to be hard," she said passionately, hoping he would accept some responsibility for the baby's care.

He said with a false laugh, "Mat, a puppy and a baby are two totally different things," figuring he could present another side to reality. "What happened to the puppy?"

Hesitant, her eyes shied away, "It eventually died." With a quick explanation, "But it wasn't from what I did, we took good care of'im, but he jus' got sicker."

"A puppy ain't a baby. You couldn't take care of a puppy, Mat, how you think you can raise a baby and with no help?" trying to establish a new maxim.

"I was hoping you would help. I mean the baby is yours." Her remark was an emotional standpoint.

"What's that look?" He was bothered by her refusal to accept the new role of conduct.

"Nothing." She understood her answer was a peaceful overture.

"No, it's something." From his voice, Seth was tired of her procrastination.

The uncertainty for her rebellion placed Seth in a new quandary between the life of the baby and the baby's death. And the choice was already made. He reflected on why she waited to change her mind.

Like always, Seth's strong point was the semblance of a problem solver. The situation was more complex than he had imagined. Evidently, he hadn't gotten through to Matilean about the consequences of keeping the baby. The friction of their choices was starting to heat up, creating a greater disturbance within Seth's smaller intestine: A throbbing, acidic pain backwashed frequently from his stomach to his throat. Things around him started to spin from a slower pace to a faster pace until his head was as a kamikaze spiraling out of control.

Seth couldn't stand any more stalling from Matilean. He eased into the cushion and focused on the center of the ceiling. With frustration and disgust acting as motivators for his attitude, he found no solace in the choice he was making. To be sure, he harassed himself for a better alternative to the set initiative, but no reasonable decision presented itself, especially not a decision that took into account his welfare.

"Damn," he cursed himself for not being able to break away from his father's grip. Even with Old Man Woodson not present, Seth could feel his father's large hand wrapping around his throat, exacting a steady and suffocating pressure. His father's ordinances were scripted in his mind, replaying over and over again like a scratched LP, sucking his courage from within him and replacing it with a fear that altered his process of moral thinking.

An expression of sympathy was divulged in blank stares and shortness of breath, wishing he could somehow explain to Matilean what he was feeling. Slavery had a way of shaping and transforming itself in many ways with familiar faces as overseers. Seth realized with each conscious look to the ceiling that his stakeholders were numerous and all wanting their own agendas met, but he was torn between two sets of responsibilities. How could he meet them all and still be in good standing with any of them? It wasn't possible. He searched the cracks and the peeling paint for his clemency and a bulwark against the disappointment he would cause to one and the pain he would receive from another. Even more depressing was the assured payoff for keeping this baby. He wanted to, but it meant further pain for Matilean and himself. Matilean was right about the baby being his, and he understood what he had to do, regardless of whom it hurt.

He looked at her forehead and thought how her deep, indented facial lines told a story of their own. It read: *Once upon a time there was a young girl who was vibrant and full of life. Her smooth skin attracted the most handsome men. There, however, was one that caught her eye. After he won her attention, he failed to mention his tradition of separation. In an act of passion there was a creation that caused internal turmoil. How she analyzed each alternative until her silky skin was a blotch of blends, and her smooth face was just a weary, worn, and weathered paste. Soon came the irritated eyes and chapped lips, sleepless nights due to spreading in her hips. In the end, the young lover's tradition was quoted verbatim and her face became a two-sided ultimatum.*

Seth had never looked so closely at her before. Actually, he was looking through her; she'd become another hindrance to achieve his underlying purpose. He had not accepted the fact that Matilean was determined to do what she thought was the right thing. His eyes wandered back into the street, now occupied by departing church members in cars and on foot.

He kept his attention in that vicinity, eavesdropping on their passing conversations that consisted mainly of church gossip. Truly, he was dismayed at all that had taken place. She wasn't going to be ignored so she attempted to distract him from those traveling the road.

"Seth, Seth."

Her persistent cry led his eyes back to hers.

"Where are you?"

"Hush now, I'm right heah in front of ya."

"Scattered 'bout in small pieces," he said, while closing his eyelids. "It's like everybody is pullin' and tuggin', wantin' me to please them, and I can't please everybody. It can't be done. Whatever I do, it's gon be the wrong thing. What am I to do?"

"The right thing, Seth. We do it together."

"What's the right thing? And by whose standard will we decide? Yours, mine, yo momma's or my dad's?"

"Ours, Seth. It's our problem and our decision, not yo father's and not my momma's, but ours."

"Well our problem affects a lot more people than just you and me."

"I know that. That's why God is gon help us."

"Damn you, Mat. Stop with all dat God, ok. All of a sudden you and God are best friends. I don't want to hea that."

It was the first time he cursed her.

He sounded like his father. It stunned her to hear him sound like his father, but it didn't weaken her fortitude. Matilean sat straight up and prepared for any other word he might say. He massaged his temples with his middle fingers. He would have preferred silence over the rambling of her solution. In his head he tallied the pros and cons of keeping the baby, and the cons won heads up each time.

"Matilean, can't you see what's gon happen? You smarter than that, baby doll." There was urgency in his voice. "Why you hurtin' me like this? Don't you know what Daddy gon do to me, Mat?" I'll be dead befo I get a chance to die in that war. All jokes aside, Mat, Daddy wouldn't hesitate to kill me if he finds out you pregnant. You don't know'im like I know'im. He clutched her by her swollen hand. And immediately she felt the pain, but she kept it from her face as she listened to his desperate plea for sympathy.

Rarely had she seen a man cry. Seth's tears tore at her heart and she saw how he tortured himself at the thought of what his father would do after having knowledge of Matilean's pregnancy. And again, she thought what her mother would do to her having that same knowledge.

CHAPTER 16

16 minutes to 10:00 a.m.
Sunday Morning

The observation of Seth's collapse led her to thoroughly think about his reasons for not wanting this child. Faced with the situation, she condemned herself for breaking him down with what she now thought were selfish motives. She was now willing to relinquish her own logic and reasoning to consider a new option to end his pain and to some degree her own.

With her good hand she wiped away his tears, expecting him to stop her at any minute. Instead, Seth was inviting, allowing her to slowly wipe them away.

"If there was no one like yo father with his ancient self and ancient traditions, you would want me to keep this baby, wouldn't you?"

"There would be no reason fo me not wantin' you to. I would be a happy man."

She pulled his hands to her chest and said, "Seth, don't you know I love you. I wanna stop your pain. I...."

Before she could finish her thought, PT's beautiful Cutlass convertible pulled up in front of the house.

They heard the smooth-running engine die down. The car door opened, then closed, and seconds later hard soled shoes scuffed the asphalt. Regaining his composure, he quickly moved his hands from Matilean's body and lifted himself from the seat. Before heading to the front of the porch, he smeared any remaining tears from his face and disappeared around the corner.

Matilean could hear the two whispering. She listened carefully to catch the words as they drifted in her direction. An unwilling moan accompanied PT's voice when Seth hadn't changed his mind.

"In other words, I am pretending to take her home."

"Yeah, and if Ophelia asks to go along fo the ride, give some excuse why she can't."

"Where should I take her once she's finished."

"Take her home. I don't know if I'll be gon or not."

"Are you sure you want to do this?"

"No, I'm not sure, but I don't have a choice."

"Are you sure this doctor is going to be there on a Sunday?"

"I talked to'im last night and for an extra two hundred he said he will. Listen PT, I only got thirty minutes befo Daddy wakes to take me to the station, so she has to go now."

PT really didn't want to be a part of it, and he was about to refuse when it felt like cotton caught his throat. It was Ophelia's voice coming from within the house. PT then realized that what he was doing was not for Seth but for Ophelia.

"Is she ready?"

Seth pointed. "She's on the side porch."

The screen door to the house opened and Ophelia came out flashing her ring. Immediately their voices died like the engine of the Cutlass.

"Hello, Nukie," she said. "I thought I heard you pull up."

"Good morning, darling. Did you dress those burns?"

"Momma put some nasty chicken grease on my neck," she pretended to whine. "And it still hurts."

"I know, baby. I'll make it better."

"Ah, hush gal, Momma said it's only a strawberry, it'd heal in a couple of days."

"Shut up, Brotha," snapped Ophelia.

While locked in Ophelia's embrace, PT gave a quick nod for Seth to retrieve Matilean so they could be on their way before Old Man Woodson or anyone else joined them on the porch. Seth dashed around the corner of the porch and yanked Matilean to her feet.

"Come on, it's time to go."

PT looked at Ophelia's hair. "Did you get all the stew out of your hair?"

"I thought I did. Why, do you still see some?"

"No, but I can smell it. It smells like she used parsley."

"Stop picking, PT."

Matilean approached the three of them. Ophelia turned her nose up and shuffled away from Matilean.

Claudia burst from behind the screen door. "Where is Momma?"

"She's in the house."

"Seth!" growled Claudia. "Daddy said send that gal home, now."

Without even being told, Matilean was already by the edge of the porch.

"She's going, PT getting ready to take her."

"Why do you have to take her?" questioned Ophelia.

"Jimmy Tops' father isn't doing too well so Daddy asked me to deliver some flowers to him."

The opportunity presented itself without him having to create a story. This impromptu lie was the best he could fabricate on short notice.

Ophelia offered to ride along.

"No!" Seth yelled in regimen command. "He can do it by himself, Ophelia."

Ophelia swung her hair over her shoulder, "I didn't recall asking Brotha's permission."

"Honey, I have to make a few more stops and one happens to be at the funeral home, and I know how much you hate seeing dead bodies."

A group of ants must have crawled up her leg because she began to scratch all over.

"Stop, PT. Go on and hurry back. You promised to take me for a ride."

Matilean looked at Ophelia's face and watched the way she carried on. What was so scary about seeing a dead body, she's already got the makeup down, she thought. She was certain Ophelia's makeup was thicker than any of her childhood mud pies that she let bake in the summer sun for hours. Matilean recalled visiting the funeral home to pay her respects to her grandmother, her mother's mother. The foundation and blue eye shadow that was packed on Ophelia's face surprisingly resembled the makeup on her grandmother's face.

She pondered if PT had gotten the makeup from the funeral home. The thought made Matilean screech on the inside.

As they were leaving, PT paused to give Seth a look.

"What?"

"You're forgetting something."

Seth thought, "Yeah."

He dashed back in the house.

"You two are up to something," said Ophelia.

"No, darling."

Claudia hadn't left. She still had a begrudging, magnifying eye on Matilean. The heat under Claudia's eye warned Matilean to retreat from the edge of the porch, just in case Claudia had a sudden notion to rush her. She could see where her nails scratched Claudia's face, but the teeth marks were well hidden with a colorful scarf.

Seth returned with the money for the procedure. It was rolled up and jammed in his fist. Seconds later, Old Man Woodson and Lillian exited the house. Without a hint or being told, Matilean was at the bottom of the steps and heading for the gate.

Old Man Woodson offered his normal frowns before saying, "Who was in the dining room last night? I know somebody was in there."

"How?"

Matilean looked off into the street; she wanted no eye contact with Old Man Woodson's cold, piercing eyes. He would know immediately that it was she in the room. That's if he didn't already know. Claudia smiled with devious pleasure. "It was Victoria, Daddy, and she had somebody with her."

He instructed Lillian to get Victoria; he didn't say a word until she came.

Before she could get out of the house, he was attacking her with his cold voice.

"What's the rule 'bout the dining room?"

She looked around the porch and the position of each person before answering.

"We're not supposed to be in it," she replied softly.

"So why was you in it?"

Victoria knew he was going to punish her regardless, and in her bones she trembled because she knew Old Man Woodson was looking for a reason to do the same to Matilean. She had already betrayed her once, and the thought of betraying her again weighed on her spirit.

She inhaled. "I plugged the stereo cord into the wall."

"Then tell me, why was the rear sliding door open? It can only be opened from the dining room." He set his eyes on Matilean.

"I don't know," answered Victoria.

Suddenly, Matilean remembered leaving it open.

"Who was in there with you?"

"Nobody."

"It was somebody." Then he drew closer to her shoulder.

Victoria's body tightened. Matilean was trying to force herself to say something, but courage refused to come out of her mouth. The mere presence of Old Man Woodson suppressed any boldness she might have possessed. She now understood Victoria's position for not telling her about Claudia's ambush. She could see everyone's fear of Old Man Woodson, but Victoria's fear could be felt in her heart as if she herself was on that porch being tortured.

"Was it her?" he asked, without looking at Matilean.

As he berated Victoria, Seth watched the infliction of pain move around on Matilean's face. Now and then, Old Man Woodson would glare hatefully at Matilean. He was unsuccessful in getting Victoria to tell him who else was in the room. Clearly in Matilean's eyes Victoria had redeemed herself. After a few more attempts, Old Man Woodson gave up. Claudia sensed his defeat and found another and better solution for him to attack Matilean—through Seth.

"Daddy," she called with caution. "I told Seth what you said but as you can see, he gon do what he wants to do."

That is just what Old Man Woodson needed to fuel his almost smothered fire. The flame in him flared from his nostrils like a raging dragon.

"Now I don told you send that nappy headed gal home. I don't want her back ova heah!"

Seth tried to cool him off, "We leaving now, Daddy."

Why don't he just come on down the steps, Matilean thought. The longer Seth stayed explaining, the more Old Man Woodson was going to blow.

He pointed in Matilean's direction. "Don't bring her black ass ova here no mo. Let her stay on her side of town. I don't want that at my house. You hea me boy?"

Seth fell back into his ounce of courage. "Ok, we leavin'." He complied by moving off to the side to safely pass his father.

It was evident that Old Man Woodson abhorred the darkness of her skin, and Seth's compliance didn't satisfactorily meet his requirements. So he began to curse Matilean and then searched for more rooms where he stored additional hate. When those rooms were empty, he pulled worse words from the basement, full of grit and soot, and slung them with an evil tongue. Matilean wondered if her sun would ever shine and end the unreachable pain that throbbed as a result of Old Man Woodson's vile words and hateful presence.

Abruptly, in the pit of her belly that caged bird sprouted its wings and flew out as spoken words, followed by a dam break of tears.

"Why do ya curse at me like I'm the scraps you feed to yo dog?" she asked courageously.

"What's the difference?"

"I'll tell ya the difference. I am somebody. No matta what you and any of yo family may think of me. I know where I's come from and I know where I's going." She looked over at Seth. "Whether it's with you or without you, Seth."

Seth felt fear rush in and grab his heart. He knew Matilean was in for it, and just as Old Man Woodson was about to head for her, Seth jumped into his path.

"Daddy, she don't know what she sayin'."

"I know exactly what I'm sayin' and I'm gon say it, and all yo daddy's hate and anger ain't stoppin' me. You is a hateful person. Why do you hate black people the way you do? Don't you look in the mirror at yoself? Or is yo reflection invisible? You ain't no whiter than I am."

"Seth, you betta take her now!"

"Go'n out the gate, Matilean, g'on." Seth tried to rush.

"Why do you hate my skin? What has it don to you or not don fo you to make you say the things you say and do?"

The fact Matilean questioned him enraged him even more. He shoved Seth out of the way and began to unloosen the buckle of his belt. He pulled the belt from around his waist and quickly wrapped it around his hand, exposing only the head of the buckle.

"I don't let my own kids talk to me dat way and I'll be damned if I let you."

Seth saw it coming and jumped in his path again. He pushed his hands out against his father's chest and locked his elbows to brace himself for any retaliation. Old Man Woodson took his free hand and grabbed one of Seth's wrists. He yanked Seth's arm. To Seth it felt as if his arm had been pulled from the joint. A sharp pain exploded up his arm. Seth screamed and gave way to his father's force. Matilean saw him coming and stood her ground.

Victoria yelled, "Run, Matilean!"

Old Man Woodson proceeded down the steps toward the gate where Matilean was standing. His anger leaped from his belly to his red glaring eyes that only the devil would know. He planned on hurting her. When he reached Matilean, he slightly hesitated before swinging the belt buckle back over his shoulder. He aimed for her face and the buckle came down hard. Matilean shut her eyes and waited for the impact to split her head and soul open.

Old Man Woodson's indecision was enough time for Seth to leap in front of the blow. The buckle cracked open his forehead and blood spattered over his father's shirt and across Matilean's face.

The door to the house opened and Edna interrupted the fragile situation.

"What's all this screaming out heah?" asked Edna, who had yet to see the blood drizzling down Seth's face.

Matilean opened her eyes. Her resolve did not weaken nor did her words. She stepped from behind Seth's protection. A steady stream of blood trickled down his forehead, flowing into his eyebrow. Then it dribbled over his high cheekbone.

Matilean caught the dark, cold eyes of Old Man Woodson and said, "I don't know what I eva did to you to make you hate me so much."

She looked to Edna who had made her way to the banister. Edna noticed the blood flowing from her son's head. Matilean wasted no time saying something to her.

"Mrs. Woodson, I wanna thank you for talkin' to me. You was right when you said God neva gives you something you can't handle. I know now that my life is much like that dust being tossed about, and like that dust, I am going to resettle." She then turned to Seth. "Seth, I am sorry, but I can't do it. I won't do it!"

"What in livin' hell is this gal talkin 'bout...can't and won't?"

Edna answered for her, "She talkin' 'bout being pregnant, Charles."

"Pregnant, by who?"

"Our son."

Old Man Woodson was about to turn the buckle on Seth's head a second time when Edna screamed,

"Charles, look at him. He's a grown man and you tryin' to beat'im like he's ten years old."

"He no man. He a boy." He raised his voice and repeated, "A boy!"

Seth had now become a rebel against his father's tradition.

"You right, Dad, I am a boy, but the courage I just witnessed in Matilean makes me wish I had an ounce of man in me. I was scared to face my responsibilities 'cause I was afraid of you and yo traditions. Those same ideas and beliefs you got was gradually becoming mine."

The blood had taken a new direction, now flowing into the cracks of his lips and curling underneath his chin.

"If me being a man means facing my fears then that's exactly what I got to do. If not now, when?" He glanced at Matilean, "I admit I am scared of being a father, but being a father will teach me to be a man."

Tears zigzagged across his face to mix with the blood. His actions held her wounded heart and filled it with reassurance and hope.

"Matilean, I want to marry you." He pleaded for solidarity.

"You ain't got to marry her!" was Old Man Woodson's cry for discord.

"You right, Daddy, not 'cause of obligation, but 'cause I wanna. I love her." His head rolled in Matilean's direction, "I'm so sorry for puttin' you through all this."

"What do you know about love?"

Seth flinched at Old Man Woodson's evil tone.

"Not much. But I believe it's time for me to learn. And Mat can teach me."

"Boy, you gon ruin yo future. Throw yo life away for dis?" He pointed at Matilean repulsively.

"She and that baby are my life. I know you can't see it, Daddy, but they are. That's yo grandchild she's carryin'. You plan on treating yo grandchild like you treat her?"

"Mr. Woodson," Matilean spoke softly, "I know you are angry." She was attacking Old Man Woodson's defense.

"You got no idea what I feel."

"I know you angry, and very cold 'cause ya had to live by your parents' rules, but don't do to me and Seth what yo parents did to you. I don't claim to know everything, but I know you got a beautiful wife, and the longer ya hold to the past, the longer ya miss the beauty right in front of you."

"Know yo place, gal," screamed Old Man Woodson.

Edna listened as soft tears streamed down her cheeks. Matilean was saying what all her strength couldn't bring her to say. Old Man Woodson turned his head towards Edna just to slice her with sharp eyes.

"Damn!" he sighed, before turning from Matilean and stomping up the steps and into the house.

Edna would never claim she understood the pain of a young, dark-skinned girl. She could, however, relate to being a young girl all alone having a baby.

"PT, go in the house and get my sweater," Edna commanded.

"Sweater?"

"It's in the sitting room on the chair."

"Where you going, Momma?" asked Lillian.

"To see a man about a horse. Seth, come on, you goin' too. Wipe that blood off yo face. Come heah so I can take a look at that."

He stood next to the top step so she would be tall enough to get a good look at the gash. "Well, you gon need stitches."

"But I have to leave soon."

"Don't worry, you'll get there." She glanced at Matilean, "Come on, baby."

"While I'm gon, Lillian, clean this heah yard."

"Why me?"

"'Cause I said so."

"I'm gon tell Daddy!"

"Tell whoever you want, just make sure you tell yoself 'cause if I come back and it ain't done, I got somethin' to show ya betta than I can tell ya."

After grabbing the sweater, PT hurried to start the car.

"Well I dos declare," laughed Ophelia.

Edna snapped her head around to cut Ophelia short of any following comment. "What do you declare? World peace?" Ophelia was too overtaken to answer. "Then I declare you to shut up fo the rest of the day." Victoria snuck a giggle as Edna made her way down the red stairs. Seth had to ask how she knew Matilean was pregnant.

"Momma, how did you know?"

"You can see it in her nose."

"In her nose?" questioned Seth.

"Well, Eddie could neva keep a secret," smiled Edna.

She made it to the bottom step when something under the porch caught her attention. "Now will you look at that, Biff gave Rimy a hair cut."

Then she laughed hard and snappishly, and looked back at Victoria.

"Victoria, call Betsy and tell'er I found her wig."

Seth laughed, "Is Eddie under there? You know he's not the smartest guy."

Like an early morning autumn breeze, Matilean felt fresh and free. When she opened the gate, she stopped to inhale the earth's fragrance. The stranger preaching was right, she thought. God had sent a storm to lift her out of her situation to be resettled in a new place with a newfound strength.

She realized her precarious walk through life wasn't going to be easy with Seth off at war, and Old Man Woodson's superficial acceptance of her. However, the internal peace the Lord had given her would allow Matilean to concentrate on one day at a time. Her dreams would stay close to her heart. If she could win today, then she knew she could win tomorrow.